...bon Twenty-Nine Vagabond Twenty-N...

Series editor: Dana Keller

The Reach of a Root

Micaela Maftei & Laura Tansley

Vagabond Voices
Glasgow

First published on 26 September 2019 by
Vagabond Voices Publishing Ltd.,
Glasgow,
Scotland.

ISBN 978-1-908251-93-0

Printed and bound in Poland

Cover design by Naghmeh Sharifi

Typeset by Park Productions

The publisher acknowledges subsidy towards this publication from Creative Scotland

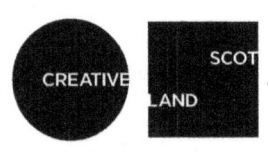

ALBA | CHRUTHACHAIL

For further information on Vagabond Voices, see the website, www.vagabondvoices.co.uk

Contents

Preface

Have you ever met someone who knows you so well they can finish your sentences? Neither have we. It's a trait often used as shorthand to suggest intimacy, closeness. But it's also a way of encroaching on someone else's voice, possibly even entering it, which can be altogether more sinister. We're interested in the meeting of the sinister and the intimate, the way one can seem like the other, or even change to become the other. In the stories within this collection both are at play, and in the development of these stories, which is to say the development of a shared voice, and the shaping and eventual sharing of that voice – these concerns are front and centre for us.

We met ten years ago through mutual circumstances (studying Creative Writing at the University of Glasgow) and mutual interests in writing and research (short non/fiction, women's voices, and the connections between self and voice). Long after the circumstances that brought us together ended, our relationship continues; we still talk to each other, almost every day, because it turned out we had other shared interests too (dinner parties that go on for too long, awkward conversations, being a non-Scot in Scotland). Professional, social and personal connections blended, and continue to blend – we connect over a piece of writing by Rebecca Solnit as much as we do over experiences with playgroups and ideas around parental leave. A key reason why this collection exists is because we knew a joint project would keep us communicating regularly, might even provide opportunities to visit each other, as well as challenging us to see where our writing might lead when we live so very far apart.

At first, writing together was an obvious way of working with and maybe even through our shared research concerns. When we turned to fiction, it was initially as an experiment. It worked well enough to lead to, at this point, fourteen co-written short stories. A co-authored collection: it's unusual to see two names on the front cover of a fiction text, we know. It's something we've been told a "real" writer would never tolerate – sharing ownership and responsibility for a text. What does it indicate? How have things been split up and then sewn together to make these pages co-authored? We can only talk about the particular process that has been used in our stories: that process is our process. The writing is ours and the process is ours, jointly, and the fiction contained here is the product of our collaborative voice. Rather than any splitting up and then sewing together, we've developed something more woven. Each story here was produced through a series of exchanges, almost exclusively via email but with niggles worked out over WhatsApp. Writing was sent back and forth, another layer of edits present each time. Rather than working linearly, we build stories from all directions, moving into each other's changes to edit the edits, rewrite the rewrites. The story grows outward, expansively, rather than cleanly from start to finish.

For all these electronic records and versions, for all that back and forth, by this point we couldn't tell you who exactly was responsible for which line or which edit. But even if we could, we probably wouldn't anyway. Why? Because we think the point of collaboration, for these stories, for us right now in 2019 at least, is not about individual ownership; at the very least it's a shared ownership. Of course, these are our stories – no one else's. In that sense we feel possessive and proud. But within the writing, we don't keep track and we don't keep score, and our numerous edits often erase singular ownership anyway. If she changes two words and I move the whole sentence to another part of the paragraph and then she puts two new words in, who is the author by the end of that? And what if we take it further than that? We of course reserve the right to change our minds, disagree and acrimoniously divorce at any point in the future. But for now we've forged a distinct voice, belonging to both of us and neither of us. So when we say we don't finish each other sentences, we're toying with you slightly; we literally do, but not in the way we would if we were writing something that was exclusively one of ours to begin with. And not in the sense of adding one voice to a second voice. More in the sense of – together, using a third voice.

Why we write together is a slightly simpler question to address than how we do it. We were, and remain, curious about transitional moments in young women's lives; about the moments when, by accident or on purpose, girls move into adulthood without really knowing why or how it's happened, or necessarily being fully prepared. As we were getting started, feeling our way into this work and these stories, we antagonised the space between, in the middle of before and after. We shared anecdotes of schoolyard mini-traumas, trial by adolescence. We recalled misunderstanding or completely blanking at the reactions we'd seen or personally experienced to our, or our peers', burgeoning sexuality. We shared ideas about shitty first jobs and the bending over backwards to try and make the impossible choice between pushing forward and risking being singled out, or lying low to keep the peace. We can trace these starting points to stories here; in "The Reach of a Root" for example, the unspoken rules of school group friendships are broken, with lasting consequences. In "Wednesdays", office politics and Marie Claire-like relationship mantras merge. In "A Change Is as Good as a Rest", we play with how a new relationship can give birth to a new self – in destructive ways that might feel exciting at first. These stories sit in the gut, exposed to and exposing the physical experience of the wavering shift between girlhood and womanhood. Together, we hope we've captured some part of this familiar and yet entirely singular feeling.

Micaela Maftei & Laura Tansley
Victoria, BC, and Glasgow

The Reach
of a Root

A Change Is as Good as a Rest

A delicious secret, a taut thrill that stretched from between her lungs to between her legs: Jess kept a mickey in her office desk drawer and her bacon bits at the back of a cupboard in the communal kitchen. Vegetarian for seven-and-a-half years, teetotal for two, a new door was opening, witnessed only by the host welcoming her in. New, new, new; everything Mark did from the kitchen to the bedroom was brand new and Jess still felt the need to hide the evidence. Too many PETA pamphlets and a household where ground corned beef was a staple meant that by the time she was twelve she'd developed the idea that true saintliness was in the mooning face of a cow, or the inane repetition of a pecking chicken. The youth worker at her family's church told her that she was bright, that she was sensitive and that if she felt closer to Jesus by not eating meat she shouldn't persist in denying herself this intimacy. He'd given her a promise and a ring on a chain to wear around her neck, neither of which were kept. But the guilt persisted: like a slick layer of spit licked on and left to dry, it tingled, insisting that she keep these new things hidden.

Mark used to be straight-edge, had a winning line of tic-tac-toe crosses tattooed inside his bottom lip when he was fifteen. He says now he's lapsed he'll get them altered by an artist, make them skull and crossbones that he'll smear with his tongue, suck with his mouth till they rouge, stretching their edges when he turns himself inside out to show them off. The questions about sex and meat and drugs and booze

3

that he used to return in the negative now get replies like "why not", "sometimes" and "if you're paying".

"It all changes when you meet someone you want to eat or smell something you want to fuck," he claimed as his knife slid through his steak, the mouthful limp with tenderness, sagging at the edges as he held it on his fork.

He flexed his fingers, making his knuckles turn white like fat. For him it was about how it made him feel: visceral, tuned.

"Oh god, it melts, it's just, melting," Jess's veal was the most expensive thing on the menu and she felt the week's wages, each calorie she no longer counted, tasting it all in an instant, churning it around and around with her tongue.

For her it was the way it made her vibrate, and how his descriptions and articulations made her feel newly, totally present. It wasn't an act either, at least not as far as she could tell. She was *there* when he talked to her, or almost there. Like a Polaroid emerging, she was a shadowy essence, and the manifestation was forming, revealing. But recently she'd been thinking of the part of a Polaroid most people forgot – the film that peels off so the image can appear. The film slots in and each picture comes out, leaving behind a black plastic sheet. That was the imprint of everything she used to consume and crave, and the rawness of what was coming out was fragile but strengthening. It was so real to her that when he talked to her or even turned to look her way, she could hear the catch, the hiss, the sliding sound as the one-time-only shot was framed, trapped and then ejected.

That night they each drank a bottle of house red, tore flesh from bones like Tudor lords, ordered coffee with cream then cognac, dribbling rich alcohol on to pristine, lacy tablecloths, their joints stiffening with crystals of uric acid. Stains from the wine's legs filled the creases in their lips and gave them dizzying headaches and spit-inducing acid reflux. Desires swelled, turning impressions into three dimensions. She asked for a plate of bacon for dessert, only half joking, and then used the heel of the bread to erase the oily juices from the oversized white plate. She fed it to him, drawing out traces of his hot mouth on her fingers after he took the bread. Where before she would have contemplated a jog after dinner, a hot shower before bed, she now looked between his eyes, focused on that less-than-an-inch, then shifted outwards to his left eye and informed him of what she wanted from him, where, which parts, how.

Mark drove a dented Datsun with two windows that didn't work and the passenger door bent down one side as if kicked by the steel toecap of a boot. She'd never asked him how it happened, it was a story from a time she was no longer interested in. She lowered the front seat until it looked like the road was coming straight through the windshield, right into her jawbone. When he settled himself behind the wheel he took his wallet out of his back pocket and put it in her lap, thick and warmed, softened leather, brown like butter heating in a pan. He drove with one hand on her thigh, speeding because he knew she liked it, the evening oiling decisions so that they happened smooth, and flexibly joined together.

Last week her flatmate tried to have a conversation about her messiness. She'd begun kicking her mail under the dining room table because it seemed addressed to another person, a different being. She'd sort through it later, someday. He'd been trying to trap her in the kitchen or hallway for days, but she barely spoke to anyone any more, didn't even answer the phone unless it was Mark. When he finally caught her he started asking about the noises he heard at night that kept him awake but that he couldn't locate.

"Sounds like rustling," he said, "then murmuring and arguing, like mewling cats fighting over meat. I can't sleep, I feel like I'm going crazy."

She didn't care if he was wound up, he needed winding up.

"Did it maybe sound like it could have been coming from outside, in the park?"

5

The building surrounded a small square of green that was supposed to encourage community but instead had become a place for owners to take their pets to relieve themselves. It was proving hard to foster friendship with your neighbours while seven dogs were simultaneously shitting.

"Maybe," he said, "have you been hearing it too?"

"Oh no, I haven't."

"Oh."

"Hmm."

"Well, if you hear anything let me know."

"Mmm. Have you sometimes been hearing a moaning, too? Like a long, low whine? Almost like a leaking seal in a pipe?"

He frowned. "Um, no. But we should put a sign up or something, get people to check. If it's a gas pipe it could kill the whole building."

"Yes, let's," and she backed into her bedroom, satisfied that nothing could stick to her, that she didn't need anything that anyone else offered these days. She didn't even acknowledge the notice in the lobby that asked residents to sign up for free carbon monoxide tester kits.

Mark was hanging on to people though, their chatter, their stuff, their stories. He liked to involve others even if they thought they weren't interested at first, liked to keep the windows open and doors unlocked. He'd invite strangers to sit with them when he and Jess were having coffee or waiting at a bar for a table to open up, or pausing to check where they were, like last Saturday.

"Excuse me, do you know where Victoria Street is?"

"Sure, it's just two blocks over," collar up, hands in pocket, side-parted hair cowlicking out of the front of a wool hat; for Mark this stranger was a challenge that made him change their plans.

"Oh great, we're looking for Tratestini's Deli," a place she'd not heard of, an idea he'd not shared, another overheard comment or notation in a paper or link clicked online, a chain of decisions apart from her, "because apparently their sandwiches are incredible."

"Oh my gosh they are," the man looked them up and down, and suddenly he was no longer strange. He took his hands out of his pockets to gesticulate his burst of interest: "You have to try the pastrami, they make it up with this soda bread that's got egg and gherkins through it. Amazing. I need to get over there more often."

"I'm an omnivore, I'll try anything," Mark said.

"What's that?"

A rat, Jess thought. An oil-blue crow. A black bear.

Mark looked him in the eyes and smiled and he was a goner, completely lost.

"Why don't you come with us? You can point out what's good," and instead of gesturing towards the deli, Mark seemed to point to Jess.

That was all it took, an appeal to people's taste, and they'd do whatever he asked. He'd say, "Take another beer, or a seven-and-seven, or a whisky and coke." He'd say, "I know a place nearby." He'd say, "How about you come check it out," and because it had gone this far with him they'd think, why not see where it all ended up? When they got sleepy he'd convince them that all they needed was some more food to soak up the booze, so they'd find a pop-up restaurant that he'd read about in *Time Out*, down an alley, in someone's flat, at the back of an old warehouse.

"So how did you two meet?" he or she or they would usually ask across the upturned crate-turned-table, the barrel, the thick glass, the granite countertop.

Jess would say, "At the circus," or "On set." Mark would smile and squeeze her hand and then tell some version of the truth, like, "We reached for the same napkin at Rachel's Bar and Grill," or "When I saw her I wanted to pull her hair up and find that place, that little hollow behind her ear. You know where I mean."

Mostly they just wanted Mark, his effusive approval, his eyes screwed up in insistence, his mouth dropped in feigned surprise. And because they wanted Mark they layered heavy looks on Jess, looks that he worked like dough, with a forearm across her chest or a hand on her ass when they walked through a doorway. One night he bit her, pretending he thought no one was looking, and she saw their newest hanger-on, Jeremy or Justin or something, bare his teeth, exhaling through them softly and then heel-toeing it over to the men's room. Jess liked the part when they left them all heated up and confused, on the street without a way to get home because they'd spent all their money and the subway was shut, she and Mark heading back to his. Under the orange streetlights and the white disinfecting glow of takeaways, these strangers stared through the situation looking for an answer or even a suggestion. She felt their confusion in the places where her skin touched her clothes.

Depending on the vibe and the encounter they might switch names on the ride home, introducing themselves to each other as the people they'd left behind, which occasionally extended into Jess shouting out a different name through the duvet in the direction of any wakeful neighbours downstairs. But in the morning the remnants were always gone, and she woke to hot coffee, minus the milk and sugar she used to weaken it with, stale bread with link sausages, and Mark once more.

The other day she'd walked past an unfinished building and stopped short at the hand-painted sign calling out to her: ARE YOU READY TO BE WHO YOU'RE BECOMING. It was either the bad punctuation or the blood-red lettering that made her eventually realise it wasn't a construction site at all but a new clothing shop, all exposed ducts and concrete floors and cashiers with razored hair and hundred-pound white T-shirts folded on steel tables. She took two bras into the fitting room – little wooden chalets with adjustable mirrors and a bench the length of her legs – then sent Mark some pictures on her phone before slinking out of the shop, using one finger to hand back the bras still clipped perfectly to their small plastic hangers.

That night they drank cocktails in a basement and met Julian, recently moved to the city and enthralled with everything that wasn't his stifling small town. Mark touched the back of his neck when he brought over a round and Julian started sweating. Emboldened, or perhaps as a response, when Mark came back from the bathroom and pronounced it cramped and red-lit, the kind of place you'd get a blow job from a stranger, Julian blushed and declared to the table that he'd take Jess up on that, though she hadn't offered.

She told him she'd take a rain check at the precise moment Mark said, "Go on then, she'll meet you there," and slid the toilet key all the way across the wobbly wooden table.

He lost a lot of his pink-cheeked air once she shut the door behind her, and the hinge of his thumb and forefinger at the base of her ear felt hard as rock.

"I don't believe it," he muttered after he came.

"Are you ready to be who you are becoming?" she asked him, easing the key out of his loosely gripped fist to unlock the door.

He threw a tantrum when they wouldn't take him home with them, and when he called out "pimp" Mark punched him in the cheek, horribly spinning his head over his shoulder. They left him with his head between his knees, wet from the seat of his jeans creeping up his back as he sat on the curb. That night Mark fit his fingers into the three pale blue marks on the left side of her neck where her hair became downy; nestled there like soft, furry fruit-bruises. She imitated his voice for Mark, sketched out his posture and movements, and fell asleep with her head lodged between his chest and his arm.

In the morning the marks were green like gooseberries, and the woman who sat next to her at work prodded them with a pen to try to elicit an explanation.

"Don't tell me, you ate too much Quorn mince and fell asleep on the remote control again," she said.

"Yeah, that's it." Jess moved the pile of overdue work from one part of the desk to another. She felt jumpy, and the woman beside her kept hitching up her tights, pulling the loose material that wrinkled around her knee-folds up towards her swollen thighs. The sound of Lycra catching on her dry skin, a hangnail scraping over the cheap polyester of her skirt, turned Jess's stomach.

"Don't you ever worry that you'll die alone?" she said. "Like, choking on a soybean with no one to, you know, slap you on the back?" and she hit the back of Jess's chair with her biro.

Jess slammed one of her drawers open and shut, stood up and clicked on to her desktop. If she didn't actually shut down the computer, most people would assume she'd just stepped out for a few minutes. She downed the drink from her drawer in the ladies' loos leaning against the lip of the sink, fast enough to make herself puke, and was back in bed with a bacon sandwich by four. But the oil lingered on her fingers, she couldn't wipe away the fat on the sheets, and she sucked her fingers so far into her mouth in an attempt to clean them that she was sick again.

The bruises were getting darker, and she couldn't keep her hands off them. Touching them produced a rash that spiralled down to her chest. Pulling her hair down around them made it limp and strained, wiped the colour from it somehow. Her annual leave stretched across another week from work, but this time she didn't tell Mark. In the mornings she put on her fitted shirt, houndstooth skirt and the high heels that hurt, left him at the bus stop and walked towards the subway that she wouldn't catch, turned a corner and took a cab instead. But secrets were oozing out of her; the bruises were brown now like *moelleux aux chocolat*. Daytime telly was distracting. Cookery shows gave her tips on smoking a brisket, how to make crisp crackling, create a blushing duck breast; looking at the veins of fat running down a shank of beef made her breathless, made her heart contract till her vision blurred and the palm she felt on her forehead was damp like a watering mouth. She ordered in sweet-and-sour chicken, meat-lover's pizzas, even ribs, then threw it all away and drank glass after glass of cold water. The next night she tried to tell Mark, ordered a salad and gave it her best shot.

After she'd explained, he watched her for a full minute and a half, and then finally said, "Makes sense, all relationships should be about compromise."

Jess couldn't tell if he was being sarcastic or not until he savagely cut then thrust a faintly bleeding hunk of his filet mignon on to her plate. The fork stayed stuck in, pointing out at an angle, and she was sure she could feel the heat from his hand off the metal. The lettuce seemed to wilt, and cheery little radishes were drowning in the protein the meat leaked. When she looked up at him his eyes were hard and his mouth was poised, and she knew he wasn't going to look away first.

Been There (Done)

The girls here are crisp, poreless and immaculate. They don't arrive till twelve because that's how long it takes to get ready, but when they do walk in they know that all that preparation is worth a pause under the air conditioning so someone can catch the wafting scent of their perfume, their possibility, the available pussy. The men are six drinks deep by then; their eyes are starting to stray and sag. I'm tall so I don't need all that performance. Being tall helps because only rich men will date tall women. Short men don't even bother to look up at me if they don't have money. But then rich men always have someone with them, would never be seen alone. So I have to lean right over when I spot someone eating a fresh catch dinner with a bottle of Sancerre, and the woman he's with has cornered him in a booth and she's speaking right into his ear even though the music isn't that loud. I bend all the way down and block the ski run that slides from her neck deep into her shirt that she's manufactured with clever stitching and starch and I smile, hand my number over and let this guy know he's got options. Everyone knows the game, or they find out pretty quick. She, his date for now, won't be mad at me in particular.

The bathrooms are hot and sticky and foetid: deodorant rolls up into tiny white balls between folds of flesh; used tampons slowly soak into the cheaply waxed brown paper bags in each stall; hairspray layers on to the walls, the mirror, the faux marble countertops. Against the clank of doors and the chorus of faucets gushing on suddenly, the atmosphere is businesslike. Everyone's going to fall in love tonight.

When I pass the table again their plates have been cleared.

For a moment I think she's scurried him away, responded to the threat by ushering him out, back to his so she can *ooh* and *ahh* at his Nespresso machine and wardrobe full of suits. But I see him at the bar buying a solitary glass of bourbon so maybe it's early enough for her to have cut her losses and gone somewhere else to try again.

He drives a Toyota with an engine that sounds like sand rattling around a tin can, but he's been living in a place just up from the beach for the past six months and he's looking to buy. He starts describing the furniture in his new office as we get in the elevator and then he fucks me in a bedroom with no curtains. One pillowcase still has the packaging creases running across it, the frigid air conditioning holding them in place. When I come back from the bathroom he's asleep, so I crack the window to feel the night pouring into the place, pooling down by my feet. The humidity rises up my legs, freshly waxed and creamy like soap lather.

There are ways to do it discreetly, to bring blood up to the surface. Tiny little things to do all day, distractions that keep the time churning. Like flossing after lunch to feel a kind of morning stretch between teeth, clean and sharp and pulsing. Sometimes I rest the hairdryer against my neck for a couple seconds, searing little kisses tender against my fingertips all day when I reach back under the curtain of what by now feels like a blonde nylon blend. Or, when objects won't do what hands are asking, a circle high up on the inner arm, points of teeth nudging in, sharp canines and the border of a molar, under a shirt sleeve, hitched up and then rolled down. Sometimes I'll carry something in my bag, something reliable. But other times I'll see something, the way an edge tapers, the precision of a corner, the slightness of something so sharp, and then I'll use that instead. Which is worse because it can be unpredictable, but the relief is utterly unmatched.

He has a potted plant, something he's bought because *GQ*

told him to, tall with a thick, woody stem and large flat leaves the shape of cupped palms that peter to a point that will give the good kind of paper cut. I lift my leg to it, test it against the underside of my foot; it scratches in a mousy kind of way. He's snoring gently, head wedged in between pillows. It's too early to check the place and get some confirmation: paystubs in a desk drawer, labels on clothing, the brand names inside the bathroom cabinet. His condoms are the kind that you can get for free from the health centre. That's either a bad sign because he's cheap or a cheap sign that he's bad. I semicircle my ankle around the razored edge of the leaf again, a thin bracelet across the bony bit. He must have nail scissors, he obviously has a manicure set somewhere, but I make myself climb back into the bed.

I'm trying to stop, because maybe the magazines are right, despite how dumb they are with their advice on worth and love and self-care. They don't understand the urge and response, the withdrawal, the unignorable prickle like scurrying insect legs. They don't understand the inherited chemicals. Or that it's a couple of things, not just blackness and frustration. It's the muscle memory, the body taking over for once and knowing how to help. It's the end result of zero bra strap rolls, a skirt flat flat flat across hip bones, a collarbone that pushes outwards, control embodied. And it's also a dark corner, a full chest of expanded quiet, and agony.

He has to work in the morning so we just drink espresso and make out in his bathroom, distracted from toothbrushing and mouthwashing for a minute. He drops me off at a café and I order pancakes, eat half whilst Googling him. He's having a lot of manufactured fun in his pictures: a couple of drinks, a couple of girls, a couple of bros, nothing over the top but his pearly whites are consistently present and correct. I could take a couple of guesses at how he's pulled it all together, curated his life, but I figure I might have an okay time finding out for myself instead of inferring and ruining it already.

Someone – from the bathroom last night maybe? – has friended me and she seems familiar, from a time before the bars maybe. Her profile picture is of salted caramel hair beached across a petite forehead, large dark eyes as big as a bat's, bright full lips. Something about her face gives me a feeling, a memory like a recurring dream of a game with string wrapped in loops around a finger, but in the dream it turns black and falls off. In the dream this takes forever and also maybe less than a minute. In the dream life races by, but always there is a string tied. Someone always says how pretty it looks, before it starts browning like an old piece of fruit. Then it grows darker and harder and falls to the floor, sometimes making a sound like it's fallen in water.

And then when I click on her and see her name I remember who she is, where she's from. It's camp. She's Natasha Linski from summer camp. The girl with the biggest twelve-year-old tits any of us had ever seen. She'd chatted to me in the toilets and I didn't realise she knew me, we all act so friendly, so when she said, "Lucy!" I handed her my lighter and lipstick like I would for anyone else.

When I met Natasha Linski I wore oversized T-shirts and a neon pink fabric bracelet on my left wrist and always took a double helping of hot dog mac 'n' cheese because they broiled it to give it crispy brown bits on top. After three weeks of summer camp with Natasha Linksi I knew that tugging your belly button in towards your spine right before the rip made bikini waxes less painful, that guys loved it when you mashed your tongue against the top of their dicks, that bras with sparkles were tacky and that chewing celery burned more calories than celery could ever contain. Natasha Linski claimed she had her period every single day for four weeks to avoid getting into the canoes, and the best moment of summer camp was when Natasha Linski told me that she could tell my boobs wouldn't grow much more, which was good because guys didn't want a girlfriend with big sloppy tits like her mum had.

I pay for the pancakes and leave. I hate seeing my own name on the credit card.

Natasha Linski sends messages with no fewer than fourteen exclamation marks in every exchange. Natasha Linski's curly brown bob has been chemically straightened since around the time she dropped out of community college. She tells me almost right away that she was recently engaged and then single again, that she's back in town and staying at her parents'. She was glad to see a friendly face last night. She's been looking for friendly faces lately. We arrange to meet up this evening, somewhere quieter where we can talk, so I spend the rest of the day chasing the right kind of orgasm, the kind Toyota withheld from me. He surprises me with a dirty text sometime around six, which is no help at all except it reminds me to get up.

Natasha Linski says we exchanged letters for six months until one of us forgot to write back. She doesn't remember who but if I had to bet I would put money on her. She was on the verge of something back then, just about to *be*. So if she got distracted in December and didn't write me I don't think I would have held it against her. But I don't really remember anything about that autumn, so maybe I'd taken my own left turn.
   "Did you stay in touch with anyone?"
   "No not really. I mean Kelly lived around the corner from me so I saw her at school but we weren't close."

"Do you remember those shitty seances we used to have?"

"I remember Judy busting our balls for lighting candles."

We slept in wooden cabins and open flames were strictly prohibited so we spent the summer lighting fires whenever we could. We'd sit around plates of tea lights and skinny tapers buried into tins of sand that Natasha Linski had stolen from the Mart in town when she'd made Camp Counsellor Judy take her to buy Tampax because Judy was too embarrassed to question it when Natasha said she only had Lil-Lets and she needed the jumbo size to cope with what she had going on. She talked about her wide hips and how hard she could take it all summer.

Natasha Linski says, "Judy was a bitch."

There weren't any other Natashas at camp that year but there was something about Natasha Linski that made you need to say both her names, like she was already a movie star that would need quoting. Over three rounds of appletinis I learn that when Natasha Linksi was engaged she lived in Charlotte, trying to break into the doctor-and-lawyer scene. The other fiancées felt embarrassed for her because her man did a lot of pro bono work, and then she admits that in the end that was a major part of how it all ended.

"Who works for free?" she says it incredulously, high-pitched all of a sudden. Then deep and down low to the table that nearly yields to her finger jabs, "That's not how I was raised. And if you do something wrong, you need to pay the price, and I don't see why I – me – should do all this work for you to avoid consequences. You know what I mean?" she shrugs.

I'm resting the top of the skinny straw right at the place where my gum meets my teeth. If I work on the pressure I can feel the half-millimetre of plastic pressing in.

Charlotte is also where she got her gappy teeth fixed, did a little forehead work for the first time and started spending as much on what she wore under her clothes as on her actual outfits. She left the lawyer a couple weeks after they'd hit the skids, and now she sighs about how hard it is to stay on top as she hunts down the money from here in Florida.

She shrugs again, "I didn't make the system, right? So I just get on with getting on and finding a man. I don't need to tell *you*, we lived together for eight months in his new-build apartment down by the water and that's gotta count for something. I mean, I can tell you what it fucking counts for. Anyway, life is tough for everyone, but my stepfather still has a boat down here and he needs someone to style it for a shoot that's happening next month, and I thought I could help him out. It's weird to be home, you know what I mean? Anyway, tell me what you've been up to staying here all this time. Tell me about your loverboyyyyyyys!" and when she holds that vowel her face changes back into the person who told me what a Dirty Sanchez was, the first person I ever heard call someone a cunt in real life.

I tell her what I know: that I've been living here and working here and working on it damn hard and I've had some good luck (a guy getting promoted pretty quickly) and some bad luck (the same guy eventually getting transferred to China and fuck that by the way). She nods along with serious sympathy; it's the kind of underenthusiastic reaction that only those that really get it respond with, head lolling low like a branch suffering under its own heavy impulse. But then I tell her about Toyota and she's back to being buoyant.

"He sounds great, like you're catching him exactly at the right time for you. How old is he?"

"I'm not sure. He could be thirty, he's got great skin. Or he could be a rich forty with a shitty rental."

"Either way, sounds ideal. Get him to phone a friend."

Double dating is normally disastrous because of the permanent risk of everyone trying to upsell each other, but I have confidence in me. I don't know mid-twenties Natasha that well but I'm ageing great, I'm all filled in and everybody keeps telling me it won't be long. So I say *sure I'll ask*, give it three days, then text something so subtly sexy Toyota responds right away, his three dots hovering on the screen for a full minute trying to match me. He knows someone who's in the city on business. We'll go out for food. Natasha replies with a link to an *FT.com* article on the Chinese slowdown and a couple of smileys that mean *serves him right*. It's behind a paywall, and I laugh because I know she knows that the idea of paying for this kind of information is somehow hilarious.

The closer dinner gets the more I feel something building despite myself. I try to fight it but eventually I text Toyota in the late afternoon and go over two hours early. I'm pretty sure I hauled him out of work but I really need something now so I blow him in the hallway of his house, looking straight down the main line of the kitchen and noticing how the chair legs line up perfectly with the breakfast bar like it's been done on purpose or styled and never actually used. Between them is a big broad way of light leading to everything beyond, the day that stretches out from his balcony windows, the night gathering itself up from nothing, to the hard ocean that's as clean as a knife edge. And it's beautiful and it's too big and it's all feeling manageable and bearable until he starts repeating "baby, baby", and then the chairs are so square up against each other and my birthday is in three months and the sun is hitting his immaculate kitchen floor at this one particular angle and it all adds up until it spills over and I dig one fingernail into my palm as a placeholder and as soon as I can I duck into the bathroom.

I left my purse in the hallway and I know I have to be quick or else he'll start wondering and I need to ward off or make way for what's coming. It takes less than ten seconds to find the manicure set I was imagining the other night and the nail scissors are so fine, thinner-than-paper fine, sinking into a spot on one hand and I get the little breakthrough, the threshold taut then giving way to a hot sweet feeling like sugary tea before it's cooled and I know it's going to happen, a sense of pure penetration and such a release that when I start to suck it clean my eyes tremble open and closed.

I don't know if they felt the same kind of trepidation but Natasha and her date are both at the bar already when we arrive ten minutes early, thirsty and needing something to steady ourselves. She's rolling a cocktail olive around her mouth, he's watching the olive. She smiles from under her HD brows and I make a mental note to take my panties off the next time I go to the bathroom just in case I need to distract Toyota or lure him away quickly.

"So I see you guys have met."

"Hi, I'm Scott," he stands and we shake hands.

"Pleased to meet you. Natasha, this is Matt," Natasha stands, they do a kind of shake but her wrist is limp like she wants a kiss.

"Hi Matt, thanks for arranging this," she says.

"Thanks for coming. So, do we need to do some catching up? How many deep are you?"

"Only a couple of fingers."

She means the whisky Scott is drinking but it's so bold, so early in the day, in fact it's still light out. So I ignore it, squeeze Toyota Matt's arm and say, "I'm just going to wash my hands before we eat, could you get me a vodka-soda? Thanks. Come on Natasha, let's go clean you up."

I don't turn round to check that she's followed; I hear her chair scrape and know she's behind me.

Once we're in the bathroom, all neutral tones and air freshener, I say, "How's it going?" first to check if she's drunk already.

"I'm good thanks sweetie, how're you doing?"

She seems pretty sober, her words roll off her tongue like she's mellow, not melted.

I test her with, "I feel a bit nervous, got butterflies."

She passes because instead of making a calculation she says, "Me too! He's cute, right?"

"Absolutely," I say. And he really is. Wherever Scott's from and whatever Scott does, it keeps him broad in the shoulders and bronzed in the face. He sort of sparkles, like water drying in the sun.

"I'm excited!" she says again, and with one hand she takes down her panties and stuffs them into her purse while the other touches up her lipstick.

I laugh and do the same.

Turns out Scott does the same thing as Matt but at a different branch, which, despite myself, comes as a blessed relief. Scott is definitely cute but he's too big for my taste. Matt is more wiry and I like the way his skin clings to him. Natasha explains to me when we pee after the main course that she loves muscles, and apparently Scott loves the taste of pussy, so they're probably going to skip out on dessert.

When the bill comes, and it turns out Scott didn't pay for himself or Natasha, I watch Matt vacillate between being pissed off and having the opportunity to show that it's no big deal to cover four dinners and a sea of drinks. He orders coffee and lets it grow pale with age in front of him.

He calls me the next day, the long, dead hour before lunch rolls around, and the only reason I don't let it go to voice-mail is because Natasha's Instagrammed a picture of herself lying in Scott's bed; nothing identifiable of course, but it's obviously a man's bed and she might as well have sent it just to me, white fake teeth blaring out of a nest of duvet, and a half-moon breast unfamiliar with gravity. She's got lipstick and eyeliner on. When he says he wants to see me and has a place he wants to take me, I wonder if this is how it feels right before it all clicks.

He takes me somewhere shabby, and at first I think he's way more plugged in than I thought and this place is about to blow up, but eventually I realise there's no irony. I'm drinking soda water and trying to figure out the point of this long story he starts telling, about how he followed his uncle into the line of work he's in and how it's not work, not really, or something about what real work is. The booths are wooden and rough, and I'm shifting back and forth along the lip looking for splinters.

I'm still itchy from the day and I want a blanket, one of those X-ray covers that presses the life out of you top to bottom. He keeps talking about his place, and the real estate prices here, and I'm totally with him for a second, but then I realise he's talking about *not* buying, and how Miami just doesn't speak to him, and he's tired of seeing everything look the same, the buildings, the businesses, the women with their spin-class haunches. He's going to the wrong class if he's getting that plastic look, I think idly as my soda warms up, and then he starts talking about the summers he used to spend in his family's cabin, in the woods when he was a kid somewhere way up north, and it starts dawning on me like an allergy, slow but rising up. He starts unspooling a lot of ideas about authentic living and tells me that he actually can't stand Scott and it's all rolling back to me in the restaurant handing over my number like someone who didn't have time for bullshit.

I can tell he's either serious about it or this is a level that I just can't play at, no one ever mentioned anything like this and I hate being caught off guard. The stupid folky music in the bar keeps dragging on, slow like syrup, and inside I feel everything speeding up and suddenly I recognise that I'm very, very late for something, or a window that's always been shuttered turns out to be smashed wide open.

He smiles at me and tells me I need to say something and it's all crawling over me as I haul him out of there and I wish the car door would close on my fingers; when it doesn't I start crowding him in the driver's seat until he actually has to pull over to the side of the road and he thinks I'm joking or playing or he's not really sure but I want to be obliterated – I start imagining lowering myself on to the gear shift again and again and that snaps me out of it; I clench up with confusion and finally see his face in front me, a wet smear on his collar and the same kind of back and forth as when the bill came. In the heavy pulse of the few moments we look at each other I press my fingertips together, a little tapping where I try to enter into the hole I made the day before. He's about to say something and I rush into the empty space, ask if he wants a nightcap at the place we were last night. Then I can feel how badly he wants me to climb off his lap, so I do.

He pulls back on to the road and starts talking about how *I'm a great person* and *really nice*. Some kind of death sentence, my caving stomach feels like, and I imagine Natasha Linski somewhere getting money jammed up her cunt, sixty-dollar panties creasing in her purse.

Still, he takes me home, and when we're outside I say, "Look I'm going away for a couple of days," spin a story about getting overexcited because I'll miss him, and when he kisses me goodbye it takes every ounce of me not to rip his lip right off, but I think I've pulled it back from some kind of brink. When I get inside I go straight to it, take an edge to the inside of my thigh and I fall into the hum of the pain, swim alongside it and then just let the current take me.

When I see Natasha the next week and tell her the whole story she crows with laughter; I can laugh too because I had some luck last night – not much, but back on the right track. She begs me to tell her again and again how Toyota phrased it, what he said, how it went.

"Did he really say *finding himself?*"

"Oh yeah, more than once. He thought if he gave everything up he'd be free – true to himself."

"Like, welfare free?"

"He said *some things—*"

"—*are worth more than money!*" she jumps in, sloshing her drink as she leans over, "and you'd be *the right one to take the journey with!*"

I've told her at least five times already how I could barely get out of there fast enough, and one time she did an impression of me that was pretty spot on, but I haven't told her how going home that night felt like blackness pouring me from his car back into my bedroom, an ink stain that was impossible to resist, so I didn't, and I had to call in sick the next two days. His texts the next day were too embarrassing to even acknowledge, so I didn't, and instead I ate everything I shouldn't, and got rid of it later, and watched twenty-eight episodes of *The Good Wife*. When we'd go out into the canoes at camp, sometimes, if you stayed still enough, you could see fish way down in the water. After rain especially the water would get pretty murky, but even then, if I stared hard enough, I could swear there were big ones gliding underneath us, and I spent so much time that summer thinking how *silent* they were. An entire life without saying one single word.

It took me a few days to get properly back in the game. I can't stand to be made a fool of, can't stand it, but my birthday's in three months. So I got back in the game like I had to, with Toyota in my back pocket. Because maybe he's the same as me: both of us would agree that keeping the moments when we're not sure at bay by doing whatever we can is key, keeps us from confusing what is *us* from everything else. And I'm maybe even a little tempted, if I'm being really honest. If he can keep my body intact and stop it slipping, stop it veering out in front of me before I've had time to catch up, then why shouldn't we give the game up? But I've heard these kinds of stories before, friends of friends who've been offered everything with nothing and I've never seen it play out in a way that would ever appeal in the long term. I want my hands to stay soft for as long as possible, get my hair soft again and let my soft face get fat, all of me rounded out from what I can afford. When I told him *maybe* he was cut up for a second, but his confidence got the better of him: his shoulders deflated but then he just relaxed right into a *your loss* attitude that he and I will both believe about each other to the hilt. We're both going to work so hard for what we want, it's just that what work is has peeled into two different pieces, like a hangnail, blue blood turning brown, or skin opening up to reveal another world.

What Lies Ahead

It's selfish and superficial, for sure, but I can't really pretend that this doesn't have an impact on *me*, and my life. Which I obviously don't mention to anyone, but it plays out in a thousand small ways. I don't take the #7 bus even though it would take me right to the corner where my flat is. And I tend to get coffee at the less convenient place, the one further from the subway, because two of the people working at the closer one are really in the least lucky, worst, unhappiest column. Repeated minor inconveniences just because of other people's lives and experiences. But I shouldn't complain; I don't complain. For me, once I see these things I can't unsee them, and they bother me, even if it's way in the future, by which time I probably won't live here, won't work there, won't be in this city even.

For me, distance brings clarity. The closer someone is to me, the blurrier the details remain. The ones I love – the ones I'd do anything for – everything about them is withheld, and I can't pick up on any dates, times, circumstances. But strangers, the countless bodies milling around in a city, can come through with electrifying volume and specificity, and you never really know whose story will be next. I sense it like a tingling in my nerve endings, only of course there's nothing really physical about it.

I haven't tried to talk to anyone, to explain it, not since primary school and Lisa Yates wanting to share secrets while we waited at base in a game of tag, which that day was an ash tree that we liked to peel the bark from. Later we got told off for damaging this tree, for flaying it alive, and Lisa stopped talking to me for a few days and that was basically the end of our relationship. She blamed me; somehow it was all connected, the tree and the secret and the game we were in the middle of and how we shouldn't have been playing on the grass. Can you imagine telling children not to play on the grass? The dinner ladies said it was because local cats liked to do their business in the sandpit that had been dug when the school first opened. I knew about Lisa after that, how she'd be an old woman, alone, alone to the very end. But so many of us can expect that. Lisa didn't understand at seven years old, that most receptive of ages, so I've never bothered telling anyone else. Have you ever been rejected for something that's such a part of you, for something that is you? Then you'll understand.

It's not like a dream exactly, because sometimes I can move around in it. My eye is not a camera, but I am a body in a space that I can't touch, that doesn't adjust for me in any way. Like I can't pick up a vase and hand it to someone. Or open a door and let a neighbour in. Or take a phone receiver from somebody and hang it up. I had a one-night stand once, really run-of-the-mill, only midway through the lights started to flicker, the smell in the room changed a tiny bit, it was a car crash, nothing dramatic or even very noisy, but a really definitive end point. No audience – just a man, wearing a wedding ring, a tree, twilight, a tiny swerve and then seven seconds later, an instantaneous shift from one state to another. Something like that kills the mood. In situations like that, it's hard not to be resentful.

The worst is the stranger that becomes a friend, or the acquaintance that integrates more and more, becomes known, becomes close, which is so easy to do in this small place. This *small* and *friendly* town. I'm stand-offish, I'm cold, I'm a fucking bitch. I've heard all the versions, but it all just boils down to self-protection. Self-defence. Sometimes I write letters instead of making phone calls because it helps to maintain some distance. Maybe that feels like it should be a new paragraph, a new thought, a different idea. But there's a connection, of course. Letters and notes and little bits of paper with key info. *The migraines are not from stress; get them checked.* That was the first, seared into memory. So indelicate, so terrifyingly blunt. It's not my fault that the message didn't work, I keep telling myself. I'm trying to get kinder, more persuasive, rather than floating around like some sort of spectre. For example, this week I tried with a ponytailed barista. I'll have to try harder, I learnt.

"Why did you leave me this fucking note?" he said.

"What note?" I tried to feign ignorance, because there's no way to legitimately explain this behaviour.

"What's the matter with you?" Hissed under his breath, because he'd get fired if his boss saw him berating a customer.

"I didn't leave you any note; I don't know what you mean. Just give me my coffee."

He took the mug behind the counter and when he slammed it back on the bar and walked away, there was an elastic band around it holding a pink, folded piece of paper against its side. It urged the use of a bike helmet and warned against brain injury following a collision. I'd spelled collision wrong.

For a while I just didn't bother. A misunderstood lecture on nihilism in a philosophy and literature module at uni gave me the excuse I was looking for to be completely lazy and just ignore it. I got fifty-three per cent in that exam, and persistent sinus infections for twelve months from popping my ears every time my vision started swimming, a tic I'd developed to remind myself of the only way I wanted to respond to

28

pressure. I'd use the library at lunchtimes, at its busiest, and just let everything wash over me in the computer labs, in the study spaces, amongst the shelves, losing sight of details and just seeing shoals of faces swirling about in monotonous scenarios that reduced to colour and patterns, the same sorts of hospital pallor, sallow blues like shallow water, the gradual slowing down of a body, or the suddenness of a forced change. The violence of violence. The agony of a slow march to a known end. It all built to a chaos, a noise without shape and without end or beginning, and really this was all a bit much at undergraduate level. I've not tried experiments like that since.

And then one day, waiting at a set of traffic lights, I grabbed a woman by her elbow to stop her walking out into the road. I remember every detail of her: tall and slim, a pair of dark-red ankle boots that added another inch to her and accentuated her long calves. A soft over-the-knee skirt in a material I could never wear because it would cling to me but it floated around her like she was waist-deep in water. Her leather jacket was undone even though it was early spring and her hair was ever so slightly wavy, effortless but utterly contrived to give shape to her long face, relaxed and romantic. I saw that she'd step out too early, following the lead of someone whose reactions would be quicker, who was more focused perhaps. So I stopped her, held her arm as the car whizzed past, and as we waited for the lights to turn safely to red we looked at each other, and although it was probably less than half a minute it felt like a much longer time. We didn't speak; her expression was blank but attentive, as if she was waiting for some vital piece of information that would let her build some semblance of what had just happened and then know how to react, but she knew somehow that it wouldn't come from me. I made myself let go of her, wanted to hold on to her for as long as she'd let me, but it would have been too hard to form a relationship from this moment. So I smiled, jogged across the road as if I had a place to be, caught up with the stranger that all too easily would have influenced her and said loudly as I walked past him, "Your actions have consequences when you're in a crowd; pay attention."

Today I leave the long-haired barista a good tip so he maybe understands my intention but wonder if it might be his own damn fault, not wearing a helmet in case it mussed his top-knotted hair. I find a table in a quiet corner of the café near a plug, away from the traffic of customers coming in and out of the front door and walking to the bathrooms. I went freelance as soon as possible because working in an office was unbearable. Now my workspace rotates, finding a balance between slow staff turnover and nowhere too popular or too tragic. I answer emails first; there's nothing except mundane admin, communications that don't even require a response, which is disappointing because boredom should be avoided at all costs.

A woman bends down to match my eyeline and catch my attention: "Can I take this sugar? I don't have any brown."

Her small mouth hangs open expectantly. Her canines stick out ever so slightly, giving her this incredibly cute pout, and then all of a sudden I can see my hands in front of me but also over her hand as it lies lightly by her side.

"It's from an old holiday," she says, which is a total blank until I realise she thinks I'm admiring her ring. It's chunky with a turquoise stone, not at all my style.

"Lovely. Yes of course. I shouldn't even use sugar."

"It's healing, you know. Or, supposed to be. Anyway, that's probably not real."

"The sugar? It's not."

"No, the turquoise!" She beams, trilling like a bird. "Well. Anyway. It's a nice memento, and if it gives some protection too then that's great!" *It won't*, I think. *Just take the sugar*, I think. I pack up my laptop thirty minutes later, because I can't concentrate, because nothing is urgent, because I figure I can try again somewhere else, because the background hum has gotten noisier and more insistent and harder to tune out. She's still there, tapping away at her phone, now-cold coffee by her arm. I say goodbye before I go, not sure why, and she looks up eagerly, like a little kid.

"Have a good one," she says earnestly, and then pats the little ceramic container full of sugar packets, the kind of awkward and semi-frantic gesture I'd make, I think.

The next day she's there again so I order my coffee to go but the barista I tried to give the note to wilfully ignores my order and hands me a cup and saucer, tells me where the milk and stirrers are, as though I haven't been here a lot, as though he doesn't know my name. I try never to think this way, but if he devoted this much energy and attention to his own personal safety, maybe I wouldn't have been put in that position in the first place. Maybe I should tell him. I don't tell him. I ignore his faux-helpful directions and turn away, balancing my saucer carefully. She's at a table next to where the chocolate and cinnamon shakers are and as I look over, weighing up whether it's worth drinking my latte without the dusting I usually put on top, the half sugar if I'm feeling especially fed up, she catches my eye and smiles. I feel it again. It's a little more vivid this time. "Does it hurt?" a voice says. "No," she says. "I'm tired," she says. I tell myself I walk over because the coffee cost £3.50 and I'm too stingy to pay that much for something and not enjoy it the way I really like it. But actually I'm scared. Scared of knowing. And not knowing.

"Morning," she says.

"Hello," I say, trying and failing to not look up from stirring the sachet into the foam.

"Do you prefer brown sugar too? I hope I didn't deprive you yesterday."

"Not at all," I say, hearing my mother in my head and the

response she gave whenever she received a compliment. *Not at all, it couldn't possibly be true.* Thinking all the while, *But yes, yes I know.*

"Mind if I join you?" I ask, which I never, hardly ever do, and there are at least two empty tables in the café, but it just kind of flows, and for some reason I really want the vision to come through more clearly. I always regret this.

"Not at all. Are you working today? I noticed your laptop yesterday," she says, while one half of my brain tracks her words and the other half searches through the fog for an image, some more words, something to pin together.

"Not today. Just a coffee and then… errands. Do you live nearby?"

Even for a turquoise-wearing believer in the healing properties of stones, this is too quick.

"Errr…"

"I just moved into the neighbourhood, and so now I'm curious about how long everyone's lived here. Sorry. You know when it's just… on your mind? Like if you break your leg and suddenly notice all the casts?"

Should've gone with cabs. Or getting a new pet. Or pretty much anything else.

"I know what you mean. It kind of awakens you to everyone else's journey, doesn't it?"

Nice deflection.

"Mm-hmm. Well so far I like it. Everything you need close by, and isn't it great to be so near the park?"

"I love it. My partner and I are there almost every weekend."

Maybe I clocked her wrong. She knows what she's doing, this one.

"So nice." I don't want to stare with the intensity I'm feeling so I concentrate on my coffee, but the thing I normally try to turn down as much as possible… I turn it way up. Make it all as vibrant, as sharp as possible. Age spots, so that's okay. Nothing too soon. But her hair is still the strawberry blonde I see now; it hasn't had the chance to lose its colour.

"Can you move this way?" someone asks, and there's a pause before they say, "Okay good… now try the other side." I know all the clues to look for – urgency in the voice? Detached professional tone? Any suggestion of a pet name or term of endearment? The dreaded "Ms"? But there's nothing much there.

"So what do you do if you're here for work?"

I stretch the truth a little bit and say, "I'm a writer, but then aren't we all."

She's nonplussed.

"Don't you think everyone in here with a laptop is writing the next big thing? That they all want to be J.K. Rowling? I know I do."

"Oh yeah, right." I've somehow managed to make this outgoing woman close up but it's okay because it gives me another chance to concentrate.

And then there it is, all of a sudden, my name rings out through the fog: *Are you Angela Clements? She has you listed as her next of kin.*

"Olivia, hi!" A woman with a brightly coloured bead necklace and bleached blonde hair waves with the hand that isn't hitching a toddler up to her hip, the one that's holding her wallet. Coins spill dramatically on to the shop counter, the floor; honestly she has so much loose change falling from her it's like she was carrying a float.

Olivia, so it turns out her name is Olivia, says, "Oh Jo," and rushes to help gather up everything she's lost while the toddler tilts precariously, head-heavy.

I drink my coffee in one go, feel it tenderise my tongue, and leave.

I was surprised to hear my own name in the vision. It's never happened before, not like that anyway and certainly not recently, perhaps because the line between stranger and someday someone known has been very distinct for the last few years. Something I've tried to maintain on purpose. This is what I get for leaning in, for trying to penetrate what for so long has been something to get the fuck away from, as Gemma Matiz so memorably told me in college after I tried to explain some version of this to her, metaphorising it by talking about career plans. She'd gotten too close, so I never saw what happened to her, although after she ghosted me for a mutual friend I spent a few bitter nights wishing desperately for the most shamefully gruesome things. No one's perfect.

I walk the streets, running over everything in my mind. I could swear on my life that I've never seen this woman before. The only Olivia I know – knew – was my fifth-grade music teacher. All the little Olivias coming up now belong to the breeders, a group I have few ties to, and anyway the timing is obviously not making any sense there. Olivia. I switch to the other voice. It was a male voice, almost no defining characteristics. No accent, no weird inflections. Calm, without being too slow. Patient, without excessive kindness. Really controlled. Exactly what you'd hope for in a medical context, only it was definitely missing the professional detachment. I head back to the café the next day, forcing myself to do so even though this is definitely not what I should be doing. *No good can come of this*, I say sternly to myself, while my hands tremble ever so slightly tying my shoes and fixing the buckle on my purse and locking my door behind me. She's not there, but I get my regular and sit at the window anyway. I take the sugars off the tables next to me, as though it's some kind of silent signal that will call her from wherever she is in the city.

I'm halfway done when she taps me on the shoulder. "I can't figure out you and your sugar. Do you love it or not?" She laughs, gesturing to my collection.

"It was like that when I got here!" I laugh back. *What a funny little world, where things just happen without making sense!*

"Don't want to bug you, but that's just too funny. Anyway,

nice to see you again," and she turns to the counter, her pocketbook in her hands.

"Wait! Can I buy you a coffee?"

"Oh, no. No, I'm fine."

"Please? I'd like to."

"Well... that's very kind. But really, it's not necessary."

"Can I just ask you one question, then? Sorry, I just feel like I really know you from somewhere. Do you know an Angela Clements?"

"Angela Clements? I don't think so. No, I don't know any Angelas."

"Are you sure? From anywhere at all?"

The air between us changes slightly.

"I'm sure. Have a good day."

"Because I'm Angela Clements," I say, because here, in his place, maybe my name might stir something.

"Okay," she says after a beat, and walks away.

I hold the sides of the chair to stop myself getting up. She gets her coffee to go and looks in the opposite direction when she passes me again on her way out.

I spend the day doing the kinds of basic admin tasks that help me to pretend I'm being productive when really all I'm doing is moving files from one folder to another, deleting others, updating spreadsheets with information that doesn't need to be recorded: real twenty-first-century, first-world tasks that are the equivalent of phoning someone to see if they received a fax. I list all the rejections I've had lately. All the companies I've contacted lately offering my services. It's distracting enough for the time being. I never anticipated being my own boss, or leading myself through the world of work. Being the one to approach people to let them know how essential I am. But I suppose I've always had direction, although it's normally been away from something as opposed to towards a goal. It's possibly why this situation has me so rattled. And why I give myself permission to, at the end of my "work day", spend time looking up local people called Olivia on Facebook. We all move in such tight circles round here, to the extent where I see the same faces moving in the same direction as me, and they're gearing up to smile at me like *hey you're the same as me, isn't that important to acknowledge* and I think *no, it absolutely is not*. But of course it's impossible, there are thousands of Olivias. Their profile pics scroll endlessly down the screen, all of them much of a muchness, all of them in their little thumbnails looking how they want to look, or really how they want people to think they look – happy, full of life, maybe a bit creative, and ever so unique. I've been so careful not to get too close that I've circled round and bumped into something from the back – that's how it feels. Trying to keep myself safe, trying to keep people at arm's distance, and somehow someone pulls me in, names me, writes down my fucking phone number or what have you. Unless I'm wrong, unless there's another Angela Clements, which I haven't thought of until this precise moment, and that sends me to the cabinet for a huge glass of wine. The thing is, I don't really want to leave. I've only been in this city for three years. It's still fine for me, and I can't keep being driven out by visions and signs. It's too early for this latte-woman to make me leave.

I can go on in this vein for hours. I know, because I've done it many times. The wine goes down, the bath gets drawn, a podcast gets layered on to the feelings that unspool in my mind, defensiveness and anger and injustice and I-never-asked-for-this. What I'm really doing is deciding whether to go back tomorrow.

In the end it doesn't matter. I see her in the street, waiting at a bus stop, checking the #7 schedule and her watch as if she has somewhere unfamiliar to be. It's a warm day and her arms are bare and she has this little silver bracelet on and it's the same as the one I've seen on a liver-spotted pair of hands, the kind of bracelet I would wear. Or the kind of bracelet I would buy as a gift for someone.

"Hello again," I say, as if it was inevitable.

She keeps an eye on her watch for a little too long before turning her head towards to me. "Oh, it's you," she says.

"Of course it is," I say, because I've decided, in that split second, to commit. "Who else would it be?"

"We just keep running into each other, don't we," she says, and there's a hair, a fine thread, stuck to her balmy lips.

"I suppose we must move in the same circles."

"Right, except today I'm going... did you follow me?" She looks at me closely, as if I'm a bus schedule that needs deciphering. "Because this doesn't feel like a coincidence."

"No I don't think it is. I think it might be something else. My name's Angela." And I can't tell if there's a flicker of recognition in her eyes, some glimpse of what's to come, what we can't control, because the breeze picks up again, covering her face with her long, fair hair and she takes a moment to peel more strands from her lips.

"Right, well. My bus is late so..."

"Where are you going? Maybe we could split a cab?"

"It's... no it's okay. I'm visiting a friend. In hospital."

I can tell this is a lie. Of course I can. Because it's what I do; I read people.

"Should I give you my number?" I ask.

"No. Why?"

"I'm only trying to help. To see if I can help."

"Really," she says, putting out both hands like I'm a dog about to leap, "just stop. I really have no idea who you are. I'm truly not trying to... hurt your feelings."

Remember this face, I want to say. *My name is Angela Clements*, I want to say, really cement it into her. *Why don't you open up a little more*, I want to say, but this last one is so over the top I see I've let this take me somewhere, somewhere unknown to her and probably dangerous for me. I try to keep my face neutral as I walk away from the bus stop, considering where to go next, which spot is likely to have tables this late in the morning. I try to scrub her from my mind as I walk, pretend she is evaporating, or at least morphing into another person. Anything to avoid lingering on the thin silver bracelet, the sharp little teeth, the unseen mouth with my name in it.

Woods for the Trees

There was a way to walk and a time to wander and Christy was disobeying the rules of both. Sunday evenings sent the city fleeing and she was mainly by herself, except for the immutable hum of hard drive machinations and signal impulses rushing up close around her and the densely packed buildings that blocked out the sky. She'd lost her way since going ground level and now she needed some kind of landmark to locate herself out of this middle. There was no need to panic, she'd try again in a minute, and in the meantime she just tilted back and let it all fall on top of her: the malls and multi-storey car parks and skyscrapers and even more massive structures behind them. But vertigo set in from looking up for too long so she let her head flop forward and leaned back against the nearest wall. There were no benches any more, no more seat-level concrete planters or soft, wooden planks, no places to encourage people to pause. Against the pressure of her body the building's nodes began to notice her. One wave every two seconds that felt like a massage through her coat. After every minute they gave off a little pulse, not a shock, as the makers and installers had been keen to point out, but a pulse. Utter mockery – such a human word for it. After three pulses a silent alarm went off; everyone knew. They dressed like random passers-by. They'd walk over and ask you where you needed to be, which was not there. Once there was a critical mass of enough buildings doing it, they all went ahead and jumped on board. Most of the residential buildings did too, especially the vacant ones.

When they were all students it had still been worthwhile to come down to the city centre, on the bus, on the tram, in taxis on a night out, for the few clubs and bars that were still rooted into what used to be neighbourhoods, resisting the higher and higher sums offered to pay up and move on. But they all graduated eventually, one by one, and then in waves, almost everyone finally packed up to other cities, with actual jobs within them. She'd come into the centre out of morbid curiosity, rubbernecking her reality.

Three pulses had passed. A woman wearing a long coat approached her, carefully casual, moment-by-moment measured, and said, "Can I help you get somewhere?" Taking a step closer the woman spoke again: "Should you be somewhere else?"

Rhetorical. Unanswerable. The woman placed her hand on Christy's shoulder, pressing down. For a second Christy thought she could grab her by the wrist and hold her hand there, feeling its shape and weight for as long as possible, but that would be contact-threat. Instead she let the woman lead her into a people carrier that drew up in front of them from nowhere and everywhere, a yellow bus for ferrying folk back out to the skirts.

"This transaction will appear on your bill as SOCIAL ASSISTANCE," the woman enunciated.

"Thank you," Christy said, because somewhere along the line she'd started thanking them, all of them.

The people carriers were given access to the riverfront roads where the views were almost exclusively for residents of one of the Tier A or Tier B buildings. White light coming from thin spots in the clouds bounced off every shimmery surface and streamed from the rear-view mirror right into Christy's face until the driver indicated right and finally pulled away from the river that she didn't get a glimpse of.

The noises from the next-door flats were so consistent Christy barely noticed them now. Each had its own tone but together they merged into a white, hovering hum that attempted to keep her company. It was like night inside thanks to her blackout blinds; the only light came from her laptop that was already glowing red with the high-priority exclamation mark of a pending payment email. As soon as she'd made a cup of coffee she closed the lid and drank in the dark.

The coffee was instant, bad. She put down her cup and stretched out her arms as wide as they'd go: one palm flat on the corridor wall and the other one on the closest kitchen cabinet. This was her flat, since she was eighteen and green. Two rooms, one toilet, and a corridor for a kitchen. She and Caroline Lavelle, best friend from college with game parents willing to be guarantors, had promised themselves at least the summer to really try to make a go of it. Back then she wasn't really sure what that meant, but now she supposed it meant life: temping, blogging, sexting with strangers. She and Caroline used to cook dinner, taking turns to sit on a beanbag chair. The space was so small – *a classic galley kitchen*, the estate agent had earnestly told Caroline's mum at the viewing – that they'd take turns boiling and straining, one of them collapsing into the foam pellets as they talked about whatever it was they used to talk about. Then they'd share a salad bowl of spaghetti with tinned tomatoes on top, balanced in the divot between two sets of knees; the corridor wasn't really wide enough for a table. When Caroline moved out she took the beanbag chair with her, and she'd wanted to take Christy too. "This place is a dump," she'd said, "you won't last another year." But Christy had just been promoted to team leader, felt unbearably pleased that she could afford the place by herself, and sometimes she couldn't comprehend the heights to which she'd risen. She was one of the lucky ones, on the inside. Or at least near to it. It was a scrappy little dank flat in a rough part that was getting rougher, but Christy was on her way and sometimes she needed to remind herself of that.

At work there was a piece of post on her desk; ominous, she thought, that whatever it was required her to have a written copy. It turned out to be an invitation to management training being held in a hotel somewhere in the city centre. She spent her lunchtime trying to locate it but the chain had so many outlets she couldn't figure out exactly where she'd be staying. Working through their automated phone system she discovered all their rooms had the same amenities anyway, everywhere across the world, so she figured it didn't really matter.

When the car came for her the next morning there was already a passenger in it. Sunglassed and stoic, she courtesy-smiled when Christy climbed in and said nothing for three quarters of an hour till they pulled into a glass-covered courtyard and the driver dropped them off at an outdoor check-in desk.

"They do that on purpose you know, drop you off right at the desk. Your feet never touch the pavement and there's no danger of anyone getting distracted and deciding they want to explore," the woman said, slinging her suit bag off her shoulder and on to the outstretched arm of a pristine porter who shone immaculately from her hair to her leather shoes. "Give her your bags too; we have adjacent rooms. I'm Sharon."

They were directed to a different lift than the one that the porter and their bags disappeared into. It came casually, giving Christy the chance to sit on a chaise longue and check out the enormous atrium which extended up through the centre of the first few floors like a panopticon. She hoped their rooms were higher up and had an outside view, but chances were if she had windows they would be facing another hotel just like this one; mirrored buildings copycatted each other across the breadth of the city.

"So have you done this training before?" Sharon asked as the lift doors closed and they headed up to their rooms.

"No, why, have you?"

"My whole section is getting trained again. We're being assessed. Restructuring."

"Oh."

"I did this exact series two months ago. But CPD is important to me. I'm happy for this opportunity."

"Okay."

"Plus I'm a fucking leader. I'm ready for this."

From floor fifteen to forty they stood still and silent until the doors opened. Sharon gestured her out and followed her down the hall half a step behind.

"463, that's me," Sharon efficiently swiped her key. "See you later," she said and disappeared.

Christy fished for her own card in her jacket pocket. Back along the corridor towards the lifts another woman waited with her back turned. Christy watched as she hitched up her skirt, turning it inside out, up and over her waist to tug at her tucked-in shirt, revealing black knickers, Lycra with a kind of lace trim framing the woman's petite butt that was perked by her black patent high heels. She righted herself, the lift arrived; she stepped in and was gone.

There was an itinerary on the writing desk in her room that said *Welcome drinks at five*, which gave Christy enough time to pace out the length of her room (same as her entire flat) and change into something smart-casual. She steamed out the creases in her shirt which had collected around the curves of her shoulders in the car, but kept her hair down. She put lipstick on, thinking she should draw attention to her mouth. She swapped her bra from white cotton to navy lace. She took her handbag rather than a briefcase, but made sure she had a pen and notepad. She knocked on the door of Sharon's room thinking it'd be nice to travel down together, even if Sharon had seemed odd, but she got no answer so went alone. The bar was on the third floor, open-planned and looking out on to the atrium. She spotted Sharon with a glass of white wine holding court with four people surrounding her. Christy watched as she spoke, saying something which made all four laugh, then leave, each scattering in a different direction. Christy picked up a red wine from a round table dressed in the company colours and walked over to her.

"Hi there, how are you?"

"Good, good. I've only been down here for half an hour and I've already made incredible contacts."

It was only ten to five. Christy had been concerned at appearing too punctual, but had clearly missed the boat already.

"I saw you talking, were those colleagues of yours?"

"What, just now? No, no. More like acquaintances. We met at a company microbusiness and mindfulness retreat last year."

"Oh I see." Christy looked around and saw them all, now in different groups, engaged in conversation with other similar-looking people.

"Watch this," Sharon said, following Christy's gaze.

Almost in complete synchronisation, each one of Sharon's mindful companions laughed, big open-mouthed, close-eyed flirtatious laughs, shook one or two hands, then moved to join a different group of people to start the process all over again.

"They'll do that three or four times, then come back together to talk about how they've read the potential in the room."

"Right."

"That's fucking teamwork."

"So they're not in competition with each other then?"

"What do you mean?" She wrinkled her nose at Christy.

"Nothing. I'm going to the loo."

"I'll join. Let's go do some power posing before the big boss gets here."

In the ladies' Sharon picked a cubicle, leaving Christy outside looking at the space between Sharon's small feet poking out under the cubicle door as she took up, Christy supposed, some kind of superman stance.

"What division are you?" Sharon shouted.

"Corporate Concerns," Christy said.

"Do you know Kevin?"

"Does he work in Eight or Twelve?"

"I don't know. I made him up. Just testing."

Christy stroked the aluminium of the faucet. It felt oddly warm.

"This has been proven scientifically, by the way."

"What has?"

"The efficacy of power posing. I'll be frank: 'You're the only one getting in the way of you.'"

Christy knew it was a quote even though she couldn't see Sharon's hands making the marks in the air.

"How do you do it?"

"Never mind. You'll pick it up on your own, or you'll never learn."

Christy thought for a second, then grabbed her crotch in Sharon's direction.

At the reception Christy tried to hover near Sharon but she edged away persistently until it became too humiliating to take a step towards her for every foot she pulled back. Christy took a glass of red instead to make herself look busy. The lights dimmed.

"You are here because we believe in your potential for greatness," announced a rapturous male voice. It was Nick, who headed Corporate Concerns. She probably should have known he'd be here and she could feel angry heat stinging at her from Sharon's direction.

"These sessions are designed to elicit mastery of the skills we've determined you have," Nick continued. "Over the next two days, we will bring it out... together. I'd like you to devote the same time and energy that I know you devote to every area of your life. We believe in you. But what we ask now – what we demand, in fact – is that you believe in yourself."

Sharon had snapped her head back to face Nick the moment he'd resumed talking, mouthing along to the words. Same script, different honcho.

Nick spoke for a few more minutes and then he let them loose. Christy put her empty glass back on the bar and motioned for a refill. The guy tending bar nodded and took her glass below the counter. Two drinks was all you got of the good stuff these days. When he returned it to her it looked the same and smelt similar, but was essentially alcohol-free. Christy skirted the newly formed groups, slinking through, circling round. She made a few crucial declarations about the potential for development in Concerns without being specific and left people nodding. By the time she'd reached the lifts she knew she'd set some things in motion and created some mystery. She didn't turn her back until she was out of sight, watching the little yellow numbers of the display count down, bringing the elevator almost to her when Sharon's hiss hit her right in the nape of her neck.

"That's a funny thing to neglect to mention."

The numbers stopped moving down; someone on the third floor was taking their sweet time and freezing them in this strain.

"Keeping that one close to your chest, were you?"

"There were rumours, but we didn't know for sure it was going to be Nick," Christy flailed.

Sharon breathed in for the entire time it took for the lift to arrive and as soon as they were in and the doors closed she spat, "Well I'm fucked. Corporate Concerns? Who cares. Seriously, what do they even do?"

"Well it's all about branding."

"No it's not. Is it? Christ, well, you're not going anywhere tonight. We need to work."

"I'm sure if you stayed downstairs and kept chatting—"

"Oh my god," Sharon burst, hands splayed in exasperation, "how are you ever going to make something of yourself? Anyway, I don't need an expert, I'm the fucking expert. I just need to skim off the top to build on what I've already got."

The lift doors opened, revealing the same long corridors evenly spaced with uninterpretable modern art and ficus plants. Christy stepped out, making Sharon follow instead of stalk this time.

"So where do you want me to start? Staff structures? Well, last quarter the Assurance Committee—" Christy let the jargon tumble, spouting strings of acronyms a foot long, and Sharon nodded along, not noticing that they'd made four left turns. Christy stopped when they eventually reached the lifts again.

"What is it?"

"This isn't our floor."

"You're stalling," she pointed to the centre of Christy's chest.

"It's really not. See?" Christy pointed to the golden 31 on the wall.

"Thirty-one is the executive floor. I thought you were taking me to his room."

"What? I don't even know him. They put us in the same car, Sharon. We're the same." At work she'd found it was generally unadvisable to take this kind of us-against-the-world tone but she tried it anyway. "You know everything I know now, I've told you it all, so why don't we just go upstairs and get ready for dinner."

When she got into these sorts of unbalanced situations Christy often found herself thinking, *What would Caroline do?* She'd throw pieces of popcorn chicken at boys she liked the look of. She'd shout at ticket inspectors when they wouldn't give her under-21 unemployment discounts on the bus. "Like I said, I haven't been in Concerns long and this event is meant to foster teamwork and strengthen networks. We all work best when we're learning together as a group." Entire sentences regurgitated, sourced unconsciously. It was appalling the way they took up residence inside her, formatting and all. Caroline would have sneered.

Sharon narrowed her eyes. "Not been in the position long? You call eight years not long? You think I didn't do my research? You're an entire pay grade above me, for no fucking reason. You've got no clue why you're here." She was getting a little spit bubble in one corner of her mouth, and now her finger was jabbing. "Let me know when you wise up," she closed, and then pivoted on one leg and jabbed the elevator button instead.

Christy turned and fled to the stairwell. It was completely silent except for the noises of a CCTV camera grinding against the bracket that was holding it up. It whirred to the left, click-click-clicked as it got stuck, unable to make its full shoulder rotation, then whirred all the way to the right. Lights for the floor above and below ticked on and off because the camera couldn't tell which direction her body was facing.

There was no way of telling if the whole encounter had been some kind of test or whether Sharon would be back down there after dinner playing a game of broken telephone, sending ripples of tension out across the room. Eight years – it felt much longer. And the difference in pay was probably to do with that. But it wasn't going to get any higher. You reached a ceiling unless you made the right relationships to move on to the next level. It was like Tetris. If you could align the situation with someone else in just the right way they would both disappear, leaving space to manoeuvre yourself. But what usually happened to people was that the shit just accumulated at a faster and faster pace, and opportunities became obstacles.

At dinner it turned out there were even more corporate guests, which upped the quality of the do from buffet to four courses and made everyone from the waiting staff to the managers still more tense. Sharon had insisted on sitting next to Christy yet refused to talk to her. The general level of anxiety was so great it started to stifle conversations everywhere, which the event organisers noticed. She watched them, Nick from Concerns and a woman she didn't recognise, rise, move over to a recess, exchange a few words then return to their table. Five minutes later bottles of wine were brought out, two for each table: an extravagance that raised eyebrows until everyone had drunk enough and forgotten to care. On Christy's table of four one was pregnant and the other an alcoholic; both went to bed early so Christy kept their two glasses topped up and Sharon seemed to forget her grudge.

"Have you lived in the city long?" Christy asked.

"For as long as I can remember."

"Me too. I had a flatmate once, she was my best friend. She moved out to the satellites."

"I've always lived alone. I love it. I've never met anyone I liked enough that could hack it. What the fuck is there in the satellites? Gardens? Guest bedrooms? Who the fuck cares."

On the inside of Sharon's lip a clot-red line had appeared and her teeth had started to stain. Christy could only assume she looked the same.

"Exactly. Satellites? Honestly. Here you're never alone but you're always alone, best of both worlds. It's great; the energy," Christy murmured, loosely tossing words to her, "no place like it. It's something else."

People still had these conversations a fair bit; newspapers still wrote about it, as though it was an actual controversy, or decision, or anything negotiable. Now you couldn't even come in from the sats without a Guidance 42 sheet, which was practically impossible to get, and going out to them for longer than a four-hour block deactivated your cityID. The intel and comms systems were different too; it was starting to be like two different languages, not that Christy really knew from experience.

Sharon stiffened suddenly and slowly put down her glass. "He's looking at us."

It was Nick, and he was looking at Sharon.

Sharon's breath had deepened, and she took her phone

out and placed it directly on the table. "I've heard of this," she said.

"Heard of what?"

"Just in case."

The phone lit up and vibrated softly. Sharon exhaled. "I'm assuming you know more about this; it's an initiative that came out of your division." Sharon's calendar had a new invitation. Christy reached over and tapped it. Nick had invited her to a strategy meeting in Room 317.

"I'm going upstairs," she said but didn't move. Then she grabbed Christy's forearm. "Is this for real?"

"I have no idea. Probably not. I mean, what kind of strategy?"

"Shit. This is time-sensitive. What's the objective here? If this is a test, what's the right answer?"

What would Caroline do? She used to throw spaghetti against the wall to see if it was cooked. When she packed up and moved out she used Christy's old suitcase for the odds and ends that didn't fit into her raft of liquor store boxes. The last thing she'd done before walking out was run her fingers over the kitchen counter and then up along the door frame, marking it. She used to rail against the initiatives and demands for "output" and measurable objectives and strategy stand-ups. What would Caroline say? *Don't let the bastards grind you down. Stick to your guns. Fuck the man.*

"This is your game," she told Sharon. Or at least tried to, but the words stuck in her throat when she saw the way Sharon was looking at her.

"You're the facilitator," Sharon said.

"The facilitator?"

"I didn't think they'd started doing this cross-level. You're a Grade Seven and I'm Six. Maybe that's why they sent us together. Did he ask you?"

"Sharon, I honestly know nothing about this."

"Why did you choose me?"

"I didn't."

Sharon drifted her fingertips over to Christy's hand. "I wasn't being critical," she murmured, "earlier, at the elevators? I was just… talking. That's not what I really think. About you."

Christy looked down at Sharon's fingers on her hand, and then over at Nick who was watching them through his almost-empty wine glass. When Sharon stood up, so did he.

"I'm going to accept the meeting," Sharon said urgently, trying not to move her lips as she spoke and staring ahead the whole time, "and you're coming with me."

They used to have a bakery on their street, Christy and Caroline, and for some reason it hung on much longer than the couple from Sri Lanka that sold individual rolls of toilet paper, or the meek-looking man who finally sold his flat to the man who owned the place next door who, he said, had been pestering him for it over the phone, over email, all the way from halfway around the world. It outlasted the post office and it outlasted the sex shop and when it outlasted the pub at the corner they started talking about how there must have been some other kind of money keeping it afloat. When they'd first moved in kids from the school two blocks down would swarm in at lunch and buy pastry and rolls and cans of drink, but then they closed the school. When the bakery finally didn't roll up its metal sheeting one day Caroline declared she'd given her notice at work, and Christy accused her of selling out.

"Societies change," Christy had said.

Caroline considered this stance a capitulation. "I'm not interested," she said.

"If you want to make a change, this is the place to do it."

"What place? I don't recognise this place."

She'd just been given her Grade Seven passcode that day. Her lunch break was eleven minutes longer than the day before. She had an elevator ID. She was on fire.

"You're going to wish you were me in two years."

"Keep bending over."

Nick's room was so large it had a living room. When Christy held the door open for Sharon she could see him at the window, rolled-up-sleeves-relaxed, admiring the view of the river that curved itself around this unseen side of the building. Sharon took her jacket off and Nick gestured them over. The woman who'd helped orchestrate the additional wine came towards them and quietly ran them through the paperwork, an almond nail gently tracing the disclaimers, holding still at the lines for signatures, and then Sharon was out of her line of sight.

"We'll access the meeting through another door," the woman whispered and led Sharon away with a gentle hand at the small of her back.

Focus. This is how you diversify, Christy thought. *Procedures are in place. This is all about mainstreaming.*

She heard Sharon's voice from somewhere: "This buy-in from the top is impressive."

Signing her initials was a confession, Christy thought, an admittance. And every word she heard afterwards was empty. She figured there were rooms along this floor with the same pattern repeating in each; people being rehoused in their own skin, unpackaged and rebranded. She felt it in the crisp white shirt gliding over skin, the cold briefcase buckle catching on nylon, the indentations in the carpet from the immense pressure of a high heel stem. Then Sharon's face was near to her again, wavering back and forth, as though underwater, between gentle anxiety and the heartbreaking excitement of a child finally invited to join a game. Eventually the two expressions swam together into something unsettling yet alluring. Her eyes only caught Christy's once after that; they stared straight through each other looking for some kind of reassurance and found it lacking.

Afterwards Christy went to the atrium, let a long set of slow escalators travel her downwards so she could look up through the centre of the building again towards its highest point. As she made for the exit another shiny porter approached her.

"Can I help you get somewhere?"

"Just going outside to smoke," Christy lied.

"Okay, well it's raining. Please take this." The porter handed her a clear plastic umbrella from behind the check-in desk. "Courtesy of Magnum Hotels."

Christy smiled and walked out of the hotel, away from the driveway, and began taking random turns left and right till she was thoroughly lost. It wasn't that late but the streets were already empty of people and the buildings vibrated with repulsive waves. It was like the feeling of standing at the edge of an ocean, with the warm water lapping in and out, eroding and sifting the sand out from under feet, pulling her deeper. She felt the city bounce off her edges and back on to itself, joined in a mutual echo.

Then, "Can I give you some assistance?"

"I'm staying in the Magnum."

"Which one?"

"I'm not sure."

"Well your ID says you live in Blue Water South."

"I'm in the city for work. Honestly."

"We have to take you home."

Christy should have realised. And there was no negotiating. Sharon would assume she'd been redistributed elsewhere in the company – or would she? What was the new normal after this exchange? In any case she'd probably become even more paranoid. But the company wouldn't mind that; they would want to keep her on her toes. She'd call Corporate Concerns in the morning and say she'd got sick. She knew someone that could forge a note. Best just to do what the city wanted.

"Thank you," she said and grabbed the woman around the waist, holding her for as long as she could before security disentangled them and sent her back to her empty flat with nothing but a bill for a body violation.

The Reach of a Root

Clare got caught looking at her cunt. A mirror between her legs, her white knickers rolled down around her knees, in the shower block of the girls' changing rooms. Ruby stood and stared, and left the kitbag she'd forgotten swinging on a peg in her wake. She wrote a long letter to Lisa about it in form, an itemised list of the irregularities: the place she chose, the look on her face, the Chanel compact tilted at an awkward angle. Ruby regretted writing it down, leaving Lisa to lay it on thick, to pass it around. Lisa, with her slicked-back hair sashaying in a ponytail; Lisa, who licked her lips in winter till they cracked, whose flat hips played tricks on all the boys who thought she wasn't ready. Lisa passed it round and Clare was never quite the same again. rosacea flushing, red thread veins pulsing, she was pink in the face forever more.

It confirmed what she had already suspected. Really, deep down, in the part of her that mattered the most, she was ugly. She would need to do a lot to make up for this huge, fundamental marking, this imposition on everyone else.

After she turned thirty, something shifted; she told herself to shift something. From then on it became more about different types of categorisation: people who knew, people who didn't and people who pretended. The first category included other women who changed in the blue-doored cubicles at the gym; the second, women who told stories of skinny-dipping and one-night stands. The third category was the most treacherous.

That was the year Clare moved to a new office. After her

parents split up in an ill-advised retirement divorce, Clare moved across the country, transferred at her own request to a new branch. She also left behind Tim, the latest example of why independence trumped headaches and someone else's post filling the hallway and dark curling hairs left in the drying bottom of the bathtub. He came up as "Time" in her phone because when he'd first entered his name, drunk, it had made them laugh so hard she couldn't change it. At first the phone had flashed "Time" far too often, until she threatened to report him for harassment and then he stopped, probably moved on to someone called Emma or Kate or Carol or Liz, some woman from the third category.

On the last occasion on which her phone had flashed "Time", he told her that people worked hard for this kind of thing and she shouldn't disregard it, and she told him she had to wake up early for a staff meeting and to stop daydreaming and believing in what all the films said. *Time is on my side*, she could imagine him singing, *yes it is*. The next day, during the staff meeting, her supervisor announced she'd be off on maternity leave in the new year, and Clare and the woman who shared a desk with her, as well as a few drinks for the past few Friday afternoons, looked at each other.

"I guess we'll have to get her some kind of gift too, once she has it," Clare said later that afternoon in the pub.

"I don't even want to tell you how many baby shower gifts I've chipped in for. You transferred to the wrong office, let me tell you. There's something in the water here."

"I don't see why you need to impose your decisions on to other people."

"We all had to go to her wedding. All of us. It was so strange. It was like, where are your friends, honey? They've been together since they were thirteen, someone said in a speech."

"That should be illegal. As should marrying the first person you sleep with."

"Mine was gay. A gay boy called Francis. His mother, of all people, had to tell me. He left me to go to art school down south and I kept coming around to his house, asking if he'd written or phoned and mentioned me. God, who *was* that person?"

"Grim."

"It used to be embarrassing but to be honest I think I got off easy. No crabs, no black eyes, no missed periods. You?"

"Someone called Robin. I'll get the next round." She reached for her wallet across the table as she rose.

Robin was Ruby's brother. He was five years older than the oldest of her group of friends, a chef in a pub that boiled vegetables to a pulp, their integrity lost to even the blunt edge of a spoon. Clare had been there once or twice with her parents, to eat lunch at 3 p.m. on a Sunday after a drive around the country. Each step on the carpet sent wafts of stale beer and fat and salt into the air like spores. Kids in the garden took turns to see who was brave enough to approach the fence that kept a dog in and the punters out.

When it was quiet, after the dinner rush, Robin would hang around in a concrete courtyard by the bins, sitting on the empty kegs and smoking. Clare noticed him there, when she asked to get some fresh air, when she skulked around in the drizzle waiting for her mum to finish her orange and lemonade, her dad his second half of ale.

"Your Ruby's pal, aren't you?" he said one day, flicking the butt of his cigarette over a wall.

They weren't really friends, Ruby felt sorry for her, but they slept at each other's houses every now and then, cooked jacket potatoes in the microwave together after school. They didn't sit together on the benches in the playground at lunch, didn't pair up in PE or mark each other's math homework.

"Well I've seen you around anyway, you're at St John's, aren't you?" He lit another cigarette, his finger curving around the filter, puffing his cheeks up with smoke, like a much older man.

"Yeah I am."

"Want one?" he said, offering her the packet, drawing her nearer to peek in and look at the contents. There was something satisfying about them lined up in two snug rows like they were. Something cute about the packet that reminded her of beaded purses that burst out of crackers at Christmas.

"I'm okay," she said, "my parents are inside."

He smiled, flicked the butt over the wall again and pulled a tube of mints from his checked trousers. He bit the top one off, paper and all, then offered her the next, his thumb pushing it out of the foil into her palm where she felt the warmth of his mouth.

"See you then," he said, and walked through a beaded curtain back into the kitchen.

Clare put the mint in her mouth and sucked it, the cold air and sugar finding the sensitive parts of her teeth. Then she climbed on top of one of the metal bins to peer over the wall; fifty, no, a hundred brown cigarette butts lay there soaking up the frost. She wondered which ones were his, which ones had stained his fingers yellow.

No matter how hard she looked, she could only find people in her life who disbelieved the truth of her earlier experience. Men who tied her hands to bedposts so that they could look at her without the traffic directions of her strong hands motioning upwards, upwards, always upwards. Doctors who swiftly closed down discussion, sending out assurances into thin air. Women who shared bottles of wine with her and, near the bottom of the second bottle, heard her words and tried to remove the outrage from their eyes.

"I think we spend most of our adult life dealing with our early years."

"I'm sure that's not true. It's not possibly true."

"Absolutely. Nuclear fallout. Is that what it's called? Everything you do and pretty much everything you think can find its way back. There's always a thread."

"Life isn't threads, it's actions. Deeds. Childhood is when you get everything wrong and nothing makes sense." She shuddered theatrically. "Can you imagine if that extended into... today?"

"Clare. Get real. Nothing *does* make sense. I mean, it *doesn't*."

"Is this the part where we blame everything on our parents?"

Her co-worker laughed, "Can you not see you're proving my point?"

"But if Ruby's parents are away, isn't there going to be anyone else there? Anyone else, responsible?"

"Her brother Robin's going to be there."

"And how old is he?"

"He's nineteen."

"He'll be in? All night? Supervising a sleepover? Won't he be out, with his friends?"

"He has to work early in the morning, at the Blue Bell."

"I'm sure he's not going to get much sleep anyway."

Clare remembered looking around at this point, at her dad, at her mum, at their plates, hers half-full of chicken skin and bones and the potatoes topped with cheese that her mum mashed with a ricer to make them smooth, like she used to like them, that took her an extra thirty minutes to prepare, congealing in the cold. They were often quiet during dinner, but there was something different about this silence, something that made the spaces between them get bigger, then contract.

Ruby's house was newer than Clare's. Everything was open-plan, the lines between rooms blurred by lighting and windows that ran the length of the house. There were four of them that night, watching drab, almost comical horror-film sequels from the far-end shelves of the video rental store that they squealed at to make them scary.

"Does anyone want to come and sit outside?"

Robin's bedroom window opened out on to a flat-roofed, shingled garage. This was where he went to smoke sometimes when he couldn't be bothered to go downstairs and out into the garden.

"We're watching a film, dummy," Ruby's face never turned away from the telly.

"I'll go."

Clare took a sweatshirt with her to put on over her nightie. She'd been snuggled under it and she tried to pull it with her when she got up, but Ruby was sitting on one sleeve. Clare tugged and tugged while Ruby first pretended not to notice and then reached under her thigh and yanked, hurling the sleeve towards her and punching the volume button on the remote so that the film drowned out Clare's uneasy laugh. She was marked now, she'd made her choice.

They sat dangling their legs over the back of the garage, looking out into the gardens of the surrounding houses, the outlines of rusting trampolines and splintered climbing frames left outside on lawns, wasp-eaten sheds full of bikes, trikes and tools.

"If you fell off here you'd break your spine," he said, and pinched the back of her neck, making her shoulders scrunch up.

"Get lost," she said, giving him a shove and a smile.

"Want one?"

"Okay."

He must have known it was her first because he lit both cigarettes in his mouth then passed one to her, saving her the embarrassment of trying to do it herself.

"You have to take it down, right into your lungs."

She tried, holding her breath with the smoke in her mouth, but it just came tumbling out of her nose like dust, like pollen.

He laughed, "You'll get the hang of it."

So they sat and she tried to smoke, and something did happen, in her head and her stomach, feelings like the drop from the peak of a swing or standing up too fast.

"Do you know how they test, to see if you have nerve damage, after you break your neck, or your back?"

"No," she said.

"Cross your legs."

She did as she was told and with his free hand he inched her nightie up over her knees, making the soft blonde hairs there stand up with the static.

"Watch this," he said, and hit her below the kneecap. Her top leg jerked up, led by her foot somehow, full of a tingle that was like when she hit her funny bone off the woodwork bench. She looked at him, quickly, and laughed. He did it again. And then once more.

"Can I try it? I mean, will it work if I do it to you?"

"I don't think you're strong enough."

She looked at her legs and wondered about nerves and impulses and then looked at the ground three metres below her feet.

"Do you know what else they do?"

"No," she said.

He leant down and picked up her foot, swinging her around on her bum. With the bottom of the plastic lighter he drew a line down the middle of the bottom of her foot. The sensation was almost unbearable, making skin, muscles, tendons, bones, everything, straighten up and sit tight till she couldn't stand it and she kicked out, knocking the lighter from his hand. She winced when it smacked the asphalt. She listened to hear whether the girls had heard it as well, bouncing off the drive, but of course they couldn't. They were too busy pausing and rewinding stupid moments, rewriting what they were watching, adding sound effects.

"Sorry," she said, eventually.

"No big deal," he said, easing another plastic lighter out of his front pocket, this one green and considerably more beat-up. He smoked two more cigarettes on the roof, and he must have known how sickish she felt because he didn't offer her another one. Her foot fell asleep almost immediately, but she was too scared to move it off his lap where he'd placed it, so she wriggled her big toe that he held between his thumb and forefinger to try to force the circulation. He wouldn't let it go.

When he flicked his last butt downwards and stood up, her foot fell heavily and she struggled with it, trying to ignore the pins and needles and thinking desperately of something to say. He helped her up with one hand and when he let her climb through the window back into the bedroom first, it was like the cars that always turned into her parents' drive to turn around and back out again – a pause, a moment until they realised it was a dead end, and then a flick of the indicator and a backwards heaving, the driver's tiny hands flying one over the other as the steering wheel twirled.

She had one foot on the sagging sofa he'd pulled towards the window as a step, and one foot on the sill. Then his hand was on the calf of the windowsill leg and she turned to look at it in slow motion. That foot had the last of the pins and needles in it, and the stubbiness of his stained fingers muted the sensation, dampened it. He looked at her for a reaction and she chose one; grinned, forgetting to smile with her mouth closed to hide her crooked front teeth.

It was only seven-thirty but they'd left work an hour early and the barman here made strong drinks. It was his own fault for telling them how much they'd save buying bottles instead of glasses, doubles instead of singles. Clare pinned her shoulder blades back against the plastic of the booth to keep from pitching forward. Her new co-worker had made a pass at her and was now probably being sick in the toilets, considering how long she'd been gone. Or perhaps she was embarrassed – Clare's reaction had not been the right one, at least not the one she'd expected. Been there, done that. Another sort of headache altogether, all it led to was twice as many toilet-paper-wrapped tampons in the bathroom bin each month, and weird looks from idiots on the street. She reached across the table for the faux snakeskin pocketbook and flicked it open with one finger. She laughed out loud to learn the woman lied about her age. There were four tenners in the billfold, and Clare slipped one out to get a cab. When she stood up her feet were unsteady, so she stepped out of her heeled shoes and carried them in one hand as she left the pub. The barman called something after her, and Clare waved backwards, leaving five sticky prints on the heavy glass door.

She'd seen herself in mirrors many times since that day in the changing rooms, when Ruby had run from her. In bathrooms, in bedroom ceilings, in tilted dresser mirrors, in consultation rooms, viewed by professionals, by trainees, by amateurs, by honest-to-goodness men and women. Tonight, as she undressed in lamplight punctuated by the gentle flashing of an answerphone message on her mobile she saw herself in twos and threes, in kaleidoscopic swirls that only settled when she focused hard on moles, scars and rogue hairs.

When her dad picked her up in the morning, Robin stood in the doorway watching her leave. Ruby was asleep on the sofa cocooned in a sleeping bag, exhausted after the breakfast they'd had at six in the morning because the sun was up and there was no point going to bed when it wasn't night-time. Clare had been given the bacon with the white greasy bits, the parts that didn't cook properly because they curled up away from the bottom of the pan. And when she offered to pour out the orange juice Ruby took it away from her, telling her to throw out the soggy carton with cracked eggshells in it that had been left to stand in a yolky puddle on the counter.

Robin smiled at her, then at her dad. They looked at each other for a moment and for her dad it must have been like dirt under his nails, meat in his back teeth.

"Who is that?" he asked, as if he didn't already know, as if there was a chance he wasn't real.

"Robin. You know, Ruby's brother."

"Right," he sounded incredulous, that this person dared to be.

Robin waved goodbye with two fingers, the rest clutching the clear lighter he must have retrieved, then turned and closed the door.

Clare's dad pulled away, fast, and drove fast all the way home, changing gears with such force, making the car chew on itself in frustration. He turned into their driveway, got out and slammed the driver door without even offering to help Clare with her duvet wrapped in a bin bag, her rucksack, her pillow. He fumbled at the front door with his keys.

"Dad?"

"What, Clare?"

Her eyes started watering involuntarily, like when she tried plucking her eyebrows. Her dad didn't notice, but then all of a sudden his hard hand was pincering her shoulder, so he must have.

"Don't bother doing that now. It's no good doing that now. Stop that. Stop it. You can't just walk around with your eyes closed like you do, stop it right now. You're going to walk into things, without realising. Don't let me catch you doing that."

He finally managed to open the door and walked in so fast he forgot his key in the lock.

There weren't enough things on hinges, with handles, with lids or on runners for her to slam shut that day. Everything was her fault: it started with her and it ended with her, and everyone else – this seemed somehow hazy and obvious at once – anyone else who happened to be caught up by her was a casualty, not an accessory. It was everything to do with her, it was backwards, it was the inside-out problem, inches deep, the length of her longest finger.

The next week in class Ruby and Lisa and the rest of them set up elaborate structures against her, invisible and impenetrable. On Monday and Tuesday, when she still carried the imprints of Robin against her, the memory-smell of his wrinkled checkered shirt and the pale hardness of his fingernails, she felt buffered, though anxious. Maybe it would be like the time all three of them had wanted those new trainers for Christmas but only one of them was wearing them the first day back in January. By Thursday she knew it was not like the trainers, it had nothing to do with them. And even though three weeks later, when school let out for two weeks at Easter, and all of Robin was completely wiped clean off her, shaved off and picked off and scrubbed away, she knew that he was still there somehow, hanging about, and she wondered how long he could exist like that, caught up in the net of echoes in the gym – flat feet, the slap of a crash mat, the snap of the door of the girls' changing room with Ruby flying beyond it – and Clare's concern caught in the reflection of a mirror smudged with her mother's make-up.

Quite Contrary

When Hannah lifted a stack of empty plant pots the burst of movement from earwigs, millipedes and about a thousand woodlice sprinting in the direction of her sandals made her fall backwards on to her tailbone, nerves prickling all the way up to her neck. She looked round to check that no one had noticed her falling on her arse like a toddler, then pulled herself back on to her feet, concentrating on her core as she did. She wanted to get stuck in and see about growing something, but it was a mess of half-heartened attempts and seasonal neglect. The empty pots were all the evidence left of plants she'd indiscriminately shoved into the ground, and along one side of the small plot were stacks of branches and twigs they'd trimmed off a mulberry tree but never cleared up or taken to the dump.

Every time she closed her eyes she saw the version she wanted to create, or, if she was being really honest, that she wanted to simply come into existence without much effort from her: cushiony moss, trembling ferns, a rustic wooden bench that B&Q probably didn't sell, sitting under dappled sunshine, which really only happened a couple of days a year in this city. It was a vision that came from design magazines and the bits in real estate shows where the host comes out into the garden to check the proximity of neighbours and how well the owners could hide from them. Garden as escape, as hideaway. But how about garden as new pub, i.e. public house, i.e. not the home? In the house she was increasingly useless, increasingly in the way and resentful of being so, increasingly slow and hesitant and tiresome. She picked up a clod of earth and pressed it between her thumb and forefinger till it burst. Did it feel like clay? Or was it softer? Should she taste it to test its pH? Did she want to eat this dirt? She'd heard that could happen sometimes, couldn't tell if right now it was curiosity or craving. She brought it up to her nose and sniffed, then withdrew it quickly as she spotted another woodlouse uncurling itself and moving towards the brickwork of the building from the tumbled tower of pots.

There was a tap on the glass of the living room window but she pretended not to hear it, picked up a trowel and dug for a few seconds just to look busy. Weeding. That's what should happen first. Just pull everything up and cleanse the palette. She began with a patch of self-seeded grass and some kind of flat-leafed green that was particularly tenacious. It had knotted itself around whatever was already growing, then periodically dove back into the soil to create another clump and a new set of tendrils that led off in several different directions. In some places it was wound so deep into the earth she wondered if it would just be easier to use weedkiller. No doubt he'd worry about the ecosystem, birds and insects and whatever, as well as something noxious seeping into her skin. Plus the minimal amount of exercise had already got her sweating and it felt good to find the bottom of pale roots thick as milkshake straws and force them away from the soil they had started to choke. She pulled up a weed, turned and found three more; pulled those three up, turned and found six more. She thought she heard a tapping again, but refused to turn and confirm this. He wouldn't come outside, wouldn't open the door and call her name. Just the tap-tap-tap, a couple fingernails on the leaded pane of glass, a beckoning.

Garden as new pub? Stupid. The old pub was good enough; no need for a new pub. No need for change, for all of this redrawing of space and rewriting of lives. She stood up and brushed off her knees and walked out the front gate before she could change her mind. She heard one last tap-tap-tap as she turned the corner to the main road, and she heard it again as she brushed her palms together to get rid of the worst of the dirt and muck. There was a limit to what you could ask of someone, she reminded herself, gears grinding as the familiar script started up in her mind, and she looked forward to the moment when his complaints and justifications would meet the first frothy cold sip and it all came together like a symphony crashing. She relaxed into the muscle memory of it all, the traffic lights changed, she began to cross. When she pushed the heavy wooden door to walk into The Red Lion, she took an instinctive look around, to make sure no one could see her, or see into her. Once she was at the bar she felt reassured by how surprisingly easy it had been to just leave. If it had been difficult somehow, if she'd had to clear up first and put the rubbish out the back, or if she'd had to get changed, it would have been less spontaneous, less urge-driven. But she could, she realised, simply walk away, because really there was no point tackling the garden without a plan. And she'd been told time and time again to listen to her body, now more than ever, so that's what she was doing. She could stand for twenty minutes, have a drink, hear it and formulate something at the same time. Although she didn't like how her hands felt with dirt under the nails. The moisture from the glass had mingled with the dried soil on her palms and made a kind of thin but slippery paste. She put a beer mat over her pint and went to the bathroom.

"I can probably stay for one more but then I'll need to head off," someone from a stall was saying.

"Yeah me too," came the utterly unconvincing response. There would clearly be some kind of entreaty between these two later, when they looked at each other across three-quarter empty glasses, *Maybe one more eh?*, and she wished there was someone she could ring just now who could drop what they were doing too and join her, but their gardens were suburban-big, required much more effort, and they would soak up every last inch of her free time with their judgements.

Hannah finished her drink and stepped outside, thinking she might vape, but even out of the side door, hovering in the entranceway, it wasn't surreptitious enough. She'd mostly switched from smoking nearly a year ago and it was fine really, but she missed cigarettes, particularly because she hated how unsubtle this new kind of smoking had become. Big blasts of sweet-smelling puff emanating around her; the long, light-up wand; the daft, digital lingo. Cigarettes were always more furtive and, as a consequence, much more appealing to her. Remnant memories of how she started, she supposed, sneaking out of the garden gate and ducking down by the back fence; or on the way home through the scrubby dingle that cut through the estate. She knew these things were all about associations, personal psychology. She wasn't stupid, or totally self-unaware. She walked a little instead, headed for one of the lanes of the main street, and stood behind a giant potted plant, looking at all the pedestrians streaming past as she leant on the wall and let the late sun hit her square in the face.

Saturday afternoons were always so busy along here. Families, couples, mothers and daughters, everybody desperately trying to produce some evidence that the weekend had happened by purchasing something, walking somewhere or eating too much. She watched a young woman who was wearing bouncy, expensive Nikes and a shimmery pair of leggings ram her enormous Maclaren pram into the ankles of a bystander waiting to cross the road, then glare at him viciously. He said, "Oh sorry excuse me," before he'd even turned round to see what had happened but once he did he seemed mad at himself for apologising when really he'd done nothing wrong. *Since when did we have to start blindly making room for this kind of thing?* she thought. The bouncy mother eased her cargo on to the road and stopped midway to say something into the cavernous pit of the pram while the lights beeped and then changed again.

She went back to the pub, ordered a half and drank it in one go, staring into the middle distance and gulping. On the way home she bought a pack of breath mints and a pint of milk and felt her shoulder blades creeping together as she turned the corner back on to her street. When she closed the front door behind her the study went suddenly quiet. She lay down on the couch, burping breath mint, balancing the milk on her stomach. They waited each other out; she knew she'd win.

He walked in with his arms folded and accused her: "You just can't sit still can you? You need to relax – give yourself a break for once."

She extended the pint of milk towards him, "I'm too tired to put this in the fridge, Alan. Will you?"

He took it, trying to hide a smile. Her stomach gurgled. From where she lay she could see none of the mess in the garden, just the neatly trimmed hedge they had paid someone to cut that gave them some privacy from passers-by. The sun had moved across the garden and was reflecting off a window on the opposite side of the street, landing a patch of warmth directly over her nose and throat, so she closed her eyes and listened to him making cups of tea (breakfast for him, mint for her). Outside she heard a car pull up; no, it was a van. She could tell because of the sound of a sliding side door being slammed shut. She opened one of her eyes. A man in a yellow high-vis vest was in her garden propping up a "For Sale" sign against the hedge. She sprang up, immediately enraged, and ran out of the flat to confront him.

"Hey! What the fuck are you doing?"

The man had already got back to the van, had one leg in the footwell of the driver's seat.

"Who the fuck are you and what did you just do in my garden?"

The man shrugged, hopped into the idling van and drove off with one hand on the wheel, the other attempting to clip the seatbelt.

"You fucking prick!"

The street was suddenly very quiet once the van had turned towards the high street and she felt self-conscious for shouting, saw her bare feet, brown against the pale paving slabs. She turned to go inside.

Alan was waiting by the front door holding two mugs: "What happened?"

Honestly, she wasn't entirely sure but she felt so incensed she forgot to be mad about everything else for a moment.

"Some guy just wedged a 'For Sale' sign in our garden without asking. What a fucking arsehole."

They both moved inside and stood at the living room window looking at the wooden pole and plastic banner. "Look! He trod all over the border. Just shoved it right into the hedge."

"Must be for one of the flats upstairs," he said, handing her a mug. "Is it weird we don't know our neighbours?" He ignored his own inane question and walked away back towards the study.

"I'm going to phone the estate agent and ask them to move it. It's our space. I can't believe he just went in there without asking us. You don't just walk into someone's garden and leave your shit lying about."

He didn't reply and she couldn't believe that he didn't seem to care. She felt so mad, her heart was beating hard. The man had moved quickly, he'd even left the engine running so he must have known he was in the wrong. The look he gave her, like *well what do you want me to do about it?*, like it was an irrevocable act that couldn't possibly be righted.

She didn't sleep that night. Just lay in bed staring at the ceiling till she got up, put her trainers on and hoicked the sign from the hedge. She jogged a couple of blocks with it then left it to rest against a park railing. If anyone asked, she'd blame students. On the way back home she sprinted, startled by a fox, and had to bend double when she reached the front door, breathing hard, trying to mentally unloose the stitch in her side and suppress the nausea creeping up.

Two days later the sign was back. She came home from work to find it buried deeper, with chunks of dirt, grass bristling out of them, lumped around the bottom of the post. When she bumped it with her hip it stayed put; someone had really planted it. She took out her phone and punched in the number on the banner while jamming her key in the front door.

"Yes, hello. Someone needs to remove one of your 'For Sale' signs that's been dug into my garden. Someone has damaged the property."

The man on the line checked the address.

"There's actually an offer pending on that property, so that sign should be gone before you know it." He was much too cheery.

"I'd like someone to come down immediately, please."

"We need to wait for the offer to clear, of course."

"And you'll need to send someone round to sort out the garden. Plants have been mangled. *Mangled.*"

"Sorry, do you mind holding? We don't really offer that service normally."

"I'm expecting a baby. You don't understand, do you?"

There was a long pause.

"That's lovely. Congratulations."

She paused for a moment, moved her phone from one ear to the other.

"I'm alone in this, do you understand? There are things I just can't do. Too much strain from heavy lifting is off the cards and I've just read about toxoplasmosis – it's terrifying."

"Isn't that the thing from *Trainspotting?*" The man's tone shifted.

"What does that matter? You need to send someone to fix this right now. It can't just be left."

"You know, from the cat. He's a junkie, well I guess they all are, but he has a cat that he's not clearing up after and there's something in the mess that kills him."

"I'd like to speak to your manager please," she said.

"I'll... if I can just take your number I'll speak to my manager."

"No I'd like to speak to them now please."

"She's not in the office right now."

71

"Does she have a mobile? I would like to speak to her directly."

"Um... please hold on for a second."

She heard the click of a mute button and the line was occupied by a soft fizz for a few moments.

"...take no for an answer... okay. Hello? So I've just spoken to my manager and an offer has cleared so the sign will be removed very shortly by one of our handymen, before you know it even."

"So your manager *is* in the office?"

"Er, no, sorry, that's a different manager. Not my manager, the office manager."

"But someone senior to you?" For some reason it was important to let this man know, if he didn't know already, what his place in the world was.

"Well yes, but they work in a different area so not really."

"So what area are you in?"

"Administration."

"Right."

"Okay."

He could pretend all he wanted but it wouldn't fool her. She put on an officious, high-pitched voice and said, "Well thank you for phoning please call again if you have any questions, we'd be happy to help in any way we can," then hung up. She hoped her tone had made his arsehole clench like when cold ocean water finally hits the waist.

On Wednesdays, when Alan had team meetings, she had about three-quarters of an hour alone after work, before he got home and created atmosphere – soft radio and bubbling dinner and a candle or two. Every other day he was home before her. Except for Wednesdays. And she'd already used up ten minutes on the phone call. She lay on the sofa with an unlit cigarette. It had slipped out of the snug pack so smoothly, perfectly, didn't matter that in less than a year the price had gone up by a quid. She'd relented and bought ten when she was on lunch and hid them in the zippered inner pouch of her purse. She'd broken the zip on purpose, so now the only way she could open it was with the sharpened tip of a pencil and a few tries. She rolled it between her fingers, stroked it, smelt it. She took a few deep imaginary drags and then inhaled again through her nose to really push it down. When it was twenty-to she went into the bathroom, opened the window, turned the shower as hot as it would go, and smoked two-thirds of it. Light-headed, she flushed the rest and shook drops of lavender oil into the steaming water until the whole bathroom smelt like an old people's home. Lavender was good for relaxation, he'd read that. Helpful for winding down.

"You smell great," he said when he got in, kissed the part where her skin met hair above her ear.

"I had a soak."

"Not too hot in the bath I hope?"

Hannah had to bite her lip to keep from responding.

That night she dreamt about weeds sprouting from her palms. When she pulled them up she saw hairy little tendrils of roots coming out of her, leaving her skin pocked and the flesh underneath raw and wet. Some of them snapped at their thickest parts as she tried to pluck at them but it didn't work and she knew she'd need tweezers, would have to tease and poke to extract them properly, and she felt the flesh pull with each bulbous tug till she split open and phloem flowed like water under her surfaces. In the morning she made a list, and asked him to go to the shops on his way home from work: *slug pellets, weedkiller, coffee grounds, sawdust.* He took the note from her good-naturedly, but concern pinched his eyebrows together.

"We should really call someone to do this for us, someone who can do it safely. That stuff is poison. It kills *everything*," he said seriously.

"To garden is to nurture," she said, "you've got to cut things down so they can grow. Again."

He sighed. "Is it really the right time for this? Summer's nearly done, anyway."

She was certain it took him so much effort to maintain this even keel, this careful tenderness.

"Is there ever a bad time to make things grow?" and she chuckled and nudged him in the ribs and nuzzled her head on top of his shoulder to break the eye contact, then started walking towards the kitchen. She knew he wouldn't miss his train, couldn't spend any more time trying to reason this through. And she knew he'd pocket the list and those things would be on the counter in a semi-transparent carrier bag in nine hours or less. She could feel the gauzy, silky plastic under her fingers now, clinging to her with static and splitting easily if her ring stabbed and caught on it in just the right way. She spat into the sink, spat again, tried to get the reflux that was generated by absolutely everything out of her mouth for once. She heard the tiny sound of the door clicking shut, closed her eyes and waited to taste nothing and hear silence and suppress the desire, growing stronger, to go out and pour salt on every crawling thing until it was possible to lie down on the ground and not have anything creeping up on her.

The sign was gone the next morning; plucked before she'd even drawn the curtains. The little chunks of grass and dirt were still upturned like a robbed grave, and on her way to work she tried to put them back in place with the toe of her shoes, patting them down awkwardly. She meant, she absolutely meant to explain the whole situation to someone at work, someone who might get outraged and share in the experience, but then she completely forgot about it, and the next day too, and pretty soon the weeks began tripping over themselves, rushing away from her, leaving her downstream, downwind, huffing and yearning.

In the evenings there was no chance to catch up; he tried to keep them busy saying things like, *You know, we really need to start buying stuff and stop getting takeaways,* and *It wouldn't hurt to get a little more set up, be a little more prepared.*

She'd reply that they needed space first, that she was still clearing out cupboards and drawers and organising her paperwork, that she was doing as she was told and listening to herself for once. One weekend he strimmed the garden to make it neat, bundled up bags of dead branches and limp roots and took them away, removing all the evidence of previous intentions. In the evenings she'd begun listening to a hypnobirthing podcast he'd looked up, but the soundtrack was so ridiculous, all wind chimes and panpipes, that it pushed her even further away from whatever it was he wanted her close to, led her towards snorting laughter and a comedic narrative, led him into the kitchen to silently prepare dinner. Sleeping was becoming a real problem, and several nights a week she'd taken to lying on the rug on the living room floor when her joints ached too much to stay in bed without waking him, and she'd end up watching whatever nonsense was on at 4, 5 or 6 a.m. He told her his sister had suggested she try sleeping with a pillow between her knees and she turned on him violently, told him his stupid sister was a whiny bitch, shocking them both into a silence that lasted until she blamed herself again, blamed her body and its invisible surging workings, a new form of begging that he could accept.

One Saturday night she sat on the sofa listening to a party happening in one of the buildings across the back close. A strong breeze blew a persistent bass line to and fro, and she toyed with the idea of complaining just to get a closer look. Eventually she went outside with a cigarette and her lighter. She mostly just held them these days, between fingers that had gotten dry and cracked. She walked down the path towards the bin shed, and a gust sent the party rushing over in her direction: synths, shouting, the smell of something singed. She followed the waft to the back of the building directly opposite, gingerly hopping over a low metal fence that separated out the different back courts. There was no back door, which she thought was preposterous, and she climbed the stairs to the second floor where a flat door was wide open. Beyond were bodies, not as many as she had expected, voices doubled by echoes bouncing off concrete and tile. It seemed reasonable to her to cross the threshold because the line that marked the start of the party was so unclear, perhaps she'd passed it already. She moved into the hallway and towards the kitchen, where a woman had her mouth under the sink tap, her tongue searching out the water but missing it completely. Instead it was soaking her long hair and staining it an even darker shade of red.

"I just... want... a drink," she said between attempted slurps to another woman who was checking her phone with long, indolent thumb scrolls, "but I can't... find any... glasses."

Ridiculously the music was cut by the sound of an advert for car insurance coming through the speakers and for a second it seemed like everyone in the vicinity paused to grasp at the reality of the situation, before another slightly slower song plunged them all back into whatever it was they were doing. As she turned away from the scene in the kitchen she almost bumped into a man who was carrying a beer in each hand.

"Whoa there," he said, looking at her belly, "easy girl, easy," like she was some kind of untamed animal.

"Excuse me," she said, and purposefully stepped to the side he'd moved to. She took a step towards him, then another, till they were nearly touching, and she was reminded abruptly about how the distance between her and other people had grown smaller and smaller, millimetre by stretching millimetre, since the spring. He stared at her, sluggish eyes trying to decipher the look on her face.

He looked over her shoulder eventually, "Okay," he said again, still smiling, more nervously now.

She took her single cigarette and put it to her lips, parting them just enough to let it slide into place perfectly.

"Really?" he said.

"And truthfully," she replied, this time letting him move past her.

Back outside, returning to her flat, she noticed someone had left a plastic jerry can on top of one of the recycling bins. She hovered over it for a second, near the nozzle that exhaled petrol fumes. The act appalled her; the disregard required to dump things and have other people clear them up, it was too much. She got closer to it, ran her finger around the opening, flicked the plastic yellow cap that dangled on its little plastic lead so that it couldn't get lost. She gripped the lighter in her pocket a little tighter, thought about how to be so silent he wouldn't hear her opening the front door and taking her shoes off, but to turn the sounds up as she got into yet another warm scented bath, so he could know the sacrifices she was making to soothe her tired bones, the aching home of her former self.

The Dinner Party

It's no big deal to have a dinner party; anyone can and I can and it happens all the time, and part of my New Year's resolution was to do it more, to do more things that are normal and fine, that normal people do, because that's what I am. Spaghetti. Chilli. Lasagne. Cheese and carbs is all it takes, really, and if you make sure to say it a few times people will remember their own booze and that's everything important taken care of. I asked Stephen to come because that's another thing normal people do that isn't a big deal, and incidentally it was related to another part of my New Year's resolution (I should maybe start saying resolutions, but I wonder if it seems better to just have one – single-minded and focused and minimalist – so anyway I can just say resolutions to myself), and Stephen *was* fine and normal about it, which made me breathe easier, like really it was fine the way people sometimes say it is, but what I didn't realise was that he would *bring Lee*, which is really the opposite of normal and fine, and not even say anything about it, just buzz me from downstairs and let me buzz him in and then knock on my door that's already opened a fraction because that's casual and low-key and welcoming and shows that I'm too busy preparing things and mixing drinks and introducing people to come open the door and then both of them are in my flat taking off their coats in the cramped hallway and actually now the whole flat is shabby and cramped and the four other people there (because Stephen and Lee are late because they're just rude; I think that's the only fucking word for it) are not pals but just witnesses and an audience who also expect a meal.

I do the introductions, include the little details, like *Stephen this is Jennifer and Matt, you met at my birthday party two years ago,* and you say the names nice and clear in case anyone's forgotten each other and Stephen can be relied upon to forget important details like names but remember ridiculous things like *isn't she the one that split up with her boyfriend after they had a threesome to get together with the other guy,* as if knowing that nugget is conducive to a good dinner party. He whispers it to me while Lee is shaking hands with them and I just smile and clench my jaw a little which I know I'm not supposed to do because it gives me tension headaches so I say, "Can I get you something to drink Lee?" because he's obviously not brought anything himself and he says, "Oh just whatever's open. A white Zinfandel if you have it," and I want to fucking kill him and maybe it shows on my face so I smile again, this time at Mike and Lauren, who I know the least but who I like the most and I want to make them feel at home. "Take a seat," I say and gesture towards the sofa but they just stand there and I think *Jesus Christ can everyone. Please. Just.*

Lee goes straight to the sofa because obviously he expects to be brought his drink, and I hate that about him, I hated it before and I hate it still, he just waits for things, waits for people to deliver, drinks and books and ideas and opinions and plans for going out and orgasms, frankly, if we're going to get into it, and he just sits and waits for you to blow him or whatever the fuck, and then doesn't even say thank you, just like right now. He's got his hand reaching out while he's still fake-half-listening to Lauren, who to be fair is probably talking about her haircut because that's what she's told everyone about so far, waiting with an open palm for "your white Zinfandel, sir" *har fucking har,* as I hand him one of the six cans of Kronenbourg Matt brought, sorry Matt. Does he say thank you? No he doesn't, he just takes it lazily and when he sees what it is, wrinkles up his nose at me and then winks like we're in on some joke before turning back to Lauren.

The wink, by the way, is a total affectation.

I go into the kitchen to get a breath and another drink because I've put mine down god knows where and I don't even mind because usually when that happens I find it when the night's almost over and it's like a bonus surprise and it was a gin and tonic which is actually just as nice if you stick another ice cube in there after it's gone warm – must make sure to remember not to use every last piece of ice on these people – and so I figure I'll go in another direction because variety is the spice of life. I pour a decent-sized glass of red from what Mike and Lauren brought because they always leave early and it's pretty obvious she's trying to get pregnant so she'll drink one teeny glass and get a headache plus it's the one with the label that's got the two bikes on it and that's really a lovely red. And I'm the host. So.

I calm down a bit when I eat a handful of crisps because I realise I'm starving, that I haven't eaten all day in fact. For hours, at least. But it's okay because the lamb needs another twenty minutes plus twenty minutes to rest so the bruschetta should come out in maybe ten minutes and I think why not, let's just eat around the sofas if people are comfortable, then move to the table for the main. Mike asks me how work is and I think about how much I really like Mike, because he's the first person to ask me any kind of personal question and I'm so relieved I say, "Great, it's going really well," when really it's not, it's awful and I'll probably be made redundant in April. And then Stephen says, "I thought work was shit?" because when he phoned to confirm this evening I'd said I couldn't talk because it was 3 p.m. on a Wednesday and the walls have eyes that are just looking for excuses to get rid of people. "It's... it could be better... but it's fine," I say. "Mine's a constant rollercoaster too," Mike says and I feel a swell of such affection I start out to squeeze his knee from where I'm sitting on the arm of the sofa but catch myself mid-reach and try to swerve towards the crisps instead but I can feel myself tipping forward so I have to quickly uncross my legs and plant my left foot down suddenly which makes a thud and then everyone's looking round. "Are people hungry?" I say, and don't wait for an answer before thrusting my hand back into the crisp bowl.

I loved Stephen once. And this thought should be jarring except his ability to be so frank was always the most incredible turn-on. "No, that's not right for me, do it like this," he'd say. "I want to put my tongue in your ass. Turn around." Okay, so maybe that's not love per se, but it's as close as I've gotten ha ha ha, and laughing to myself inside my own head means it takes me a second to realise that I'm probably right, and it is the closest I've gotten to love even though to be fair you really should've heard his tone when he said those things, tone counts for a lot, but anyway, that feels like something I should spend some time being sad about. Later, though. So I do pat Mike's knee but now it's been a minute or so and he's in the middle of talking to Lauren, his actual girlfriend who is sitting right beside him, and thank god he's a decent human being who, instead of staring at me, pats me back but also at the end of the final tap eases my hand off his knee without being obvious. I announce to the room that I'm just going to fetch the starter and head to the kitchen to perform the final drizzle of oil over the bruschetta. It's not right to serve something you haven't tried so I take a big bite of one slice, which I have to say looks gorgeous, not bragging, just glad I splurged on the deli bruschetta mix instead of chopping all those tomatoes up myself because they're all little uniform squares and that's when Lee decides to walk in and open my fridge likes he owns the place. "So, first off, you didn't bring anything to drink, and second, you shouldn't be here," I say. "What, in the kitchen? Too late, caught you snacking." He sings it like a playground rhyme. "No I mean here, here. Tonight." "Stephen asked me." He picks at something in his teeth I certainly haven't served with his little fingernail. "Stephen can't ask you to *my* house." He holds up one hand. "Your room-mate doing a semester abroad does not somehow turn this flat into your own house." It's so lucky with Vickie going to Barcelona for literally months and her parents being rich enough that they don't care about paying rent still, really it can't be better. And I keep this place nice, I hang pictures. But anyway I don't want to get sidetracked. Lee takes out the bottle of organic papaya-and-orange juice that Lauren brought to drink once her three ounces of wine makes her a little bit nauseous and she remembers how important folic acid is during preconception. "That's Lauren's," I hiss, but he's twisted the top off already. "Just get out, Lee!" Then he says, "If I'm being honest, I should tell you that Stephen told me you'd be very happy if I came." Bastard. Both of them, or whichever is lying, or maybe both of them. "I've never been happy any single time you've come," I say, marching out of the kitchen with the platter which I only notice still has the half-eaten bruschetta on it right around the time everyone else does too. Then I hear Lee playing around with the oven, which is really the last straw and I try to ignore it only he calls out, "I think there's a timer going off," and I remember the fucking lamb. "Help yourselves," I say and put down the bruschetta, "sorry, a little mouse has been at that one," and no one laughs and I wonder do these people really think that I live in such a way that a mouse might be an actual possibility? So I laugh and say, "Did a taste test, chef's prerogative!" Mike says, "Quite right," and leans over to take a piece but maybe without noticing the chirpy red napkins I've laid out to help us be informal around the sofas and when he takes a bite crispy bread collapses in his teeth, sprinkling tomato and crumbs and whatever dressing all over the carpet. He looks embarrassed and I can't bear to look so I pretend I haven't seen and head back to the kitchen.

Lee is still fucking around with the oven and holding the juice. "I've got it, thanks. Just go and sit down." "Fine, fine," he says and then from the living room I hear him say, "You don't mind sharing do you Lauren?" and I know Stephen has probably told him the threesome story. At least the lamb looks lovely. The herb crust looks like a soft moss covering a woodland log and when I poke the middle with a knife it slides in and out like it's moving through candyfloss or a sponge cake and only a little bit of blood bubbles up to the surface and the blade is hot. Get it fucking down you, you slobs, you don't deserve my lamb. Except maybe Mike.

Jennifer pokes her head through the breakfast nook and says, "Can I do anything to help?" and I know she's just having a nosy but that's fine because I want her to know how brilliant the lamb looks sitting like it is, proud and whole in the baking tray, before I slice it up to serve. "That's okay, just needs to rest now. Have you had some bruschetta?" I say. "I'm actually allergic to tomatoes," she says. "Ha ha," I say. Then, "You're not. Are you?" "Well," she holds my eye contact, "it's a recent thing, I come out in a rash." *For. God's. Sake.* "Oh dear," I say. "Sorry, I should have texted you," she says. *Yes you fucking should have* I think. "Yes you fucking should have," I say because Jennifer will know that I'm joking but actually it seems like not really. Oh well, that's fine, too late. "Can you cope with just crisps for now? Or there's a spare bit of bread here?" She moves into the kitchen and takes the end of the bread that's left on the counter, puts her thumb over the top of the olive oil and lets a stream douse it for a second:

"Why is Lee here?" she says. "Don't even get me started," I start, because Jennifer has heard my opinion on every angle of Lee. "Do you ever, like, look at two people and wonder what on earth it is they talk about? Like, how they pass the time together?" I say. "Yes, yes I do. Wait, which two?" she says, and I try to backtrack. "Any two. I mean, many twos." But then maybe she thinks I'm talking about her and Matt because of Matt's plasterboard personality. "Like opposites attract but they don't?" she says. "Yes," I say. "Some people should just... physically repel each other. Like magnets." "Bread's lovely," she muses in a wistful way. "Look, I tried to tell him to leave." "Here," she says, bravely putting on the oven mitts I've left on the counter, "let me help you take that out." I nearly laugh out loud. As if she's going to fucking walk in there with my lamb, putting it down on the table like some kind of pioneer woman sharer of bounty. Little cunt. "I'm fine. If you want you could bring the salad from the fridge though?" With two dishcloths I grab the side of the ovenproof dish and shout, "Oi you hungry bastards! Dinner time!" in a cheery tone.

Here we go. We're nearly half done now I'd say.

At the table everyone serves themselves with gusto. I notice someone's trod all over the bits of bruschetta mix that Mike spilt. Vickie won't be pleased. I wonder what takes out tomato stains. White wine and soda water? It's Stephen who starts it off. "What kind of lamb is this?" he asks. "Lamb. From Hudson's, d'you know it?" I say sweetly. Hudson's is the new posh butcher that sells bacon for four times the price in Tesco and tells you how happy the pigs were. One of the last nights Lee came round he had two pies from there that were to be fair absolutely ridiculous and when he told me how much they cost I hit him. "Yep, I know Hudson's, but what the fuck was it raised on?" He's making me nervous, and still chewing his first mouthful. "Erm, probably clover and mother's milk?" I venture, sawing off a gorgeous-looking chunk. But as soon as it hits my tongue I taste dirt. It tastes like dirt that's been smothered in mustard. Sticks and wet leaves and a dusty kind of rot, all covered with something like burning. Goddamn you Nigella.

I wondered later if I could ever be the kind of person to laugh it off, be in on the joke for once, and what the kind of person that could laugh it off would be like to hang out with in real life, and I realised I wouldn't like her, so that's why when Mike said, "Grass-fed, probably, it tastes really... organic," I just nodded and kept everyone's glasses topped up because if you invite people round for dinner it's reasonable to expect to be satiated. So no one had seconds of the meat but they ate all the potatoes and I'd been sure to make extra because everyone loves Hasselback potatoes, the way they look like dinosaur vertebrae or burning logs, dripping with butter; they were delicious and I made sure to say it at least twice. Everyone agreed and I knew they weren't lying and even Stephen nodded enthusiastically with one cheek full and his eyes all wide like he couldn't believe it was possible I was responsible for what was going on in his mouth.

When Stephen and I broke up I used to log into his emails just because I knew his password. I never found anything that was worth the effort except two half-finished messages in his drafts folder that didn't mention me specifically but were clearly for me or about me and I kept an eye on these, waiting for them to become sent messages, but they never did, and the last time I logged on I got a notification saying someone was logged in at another location, and I knew he would have got that notification too, with a warning to increase his security settings. He changed his password after that, and he must have known it was me. I think everyone can agree that breaking up makes for bad decisions. And all I want now is for him to know that I'm not that person any more, that he's just not that interesting. Except I watch everyone round the table hang on his every word as he tells the story of the time he got himself upgraded on a plane and Lee looks pissed about this story, which means that when Stephen says, "And so we take these two really cheap Primark ties and put them on with our polo shirts, take our socks off and roll up our slacks, keep our sunglasses on the entire time and everyone thinks we're fucking DJs or something, people start taking our photos," the "we" and "our" doesn't include him. The angrier he gets the more annoyed I feel with him, but underneath that there's a kind of sick kinship. I can see into the future, I think, see myself portioning out the mousse I made earlier this afternoon, who the hell cares any more if it set properly or not, and everyone getting ready to go at some early time when I'm not ready to stop, with Lauren cradling her wan face in her porcelain hand, apologetic, and I'll pour myself another huge glass of whatever's left lying around, whatever dregs and scraps people are too embarrassed to pack up and take with them, and if Lee texts a couple hours later I'll probably reply or even be the one who texts, to be honest, even after the last time where he pretended not to know it was me texting him. Is it a more authentic hate-fuck if it's yourself you hate?

I'm so engrossed in fast-forwarding the movie I'm watching in my mind that I hardly notice when Mike starts stacking plates, which is hard to do because each plate still has a medium-to-large-sized chunk of lamb on it, but bless him he's making it work. And even though it's my place I let him take them all into the kitchen and clatter around, but when Lauren calls out asking him to bring out her juice I half get up to go help somehow, or try and find some other juice, and

86

when I see Lee sipping it I basically want to kill him again. Stephen thinks it's a good idea that we're getting together and that's probably part of the reason why I'm doing it, and he thinks Lee is the kind of person that should be judged by what he does not what he says and what he does is fuck me every so often, late at night when he feels less restrained, and so when we do it we rarely do it in a bed and I think about absolutely nothing else when it's happening and it's lucky that Vickie isn't around to trip over us when she goes to the bathroom in the middle of the night. Tonight feels different though; tonight feels like the kind of night when I'll know if we're doing it on the spot where Mike spilt the bruschetta and then I'll be thinking about crumbs and thick pile and stains and the time when I was twelve and we were on holiday in France and I got really sunburnt so my dad rubbed tomatoes on my legs and at first it stung but then it settled into this warm hum and he let me sleep outside in the hammock so I could be cool even though when I was older he told me he'd worried all night that I'd be abducted.

"Lee, could you please pour some of that juice for Lauren?" I say as the bottle reaches his lips and Lauren looks round at him, horrified. "It's fine, don't worry about it," she says, "I'll have water." And she calls out, "Mike, could you get me some water?" Lee just smiles, then continues to drink. Mike doesn't immediately come out of the kitchen with a glass so Lauren stands up and says, "Actually I'm quite tired, and Mike has an early start in the morning so we might just head," and the night is collapsing so I follow Lauren into the kitchen.

Mike has stacked the plates in a perfectly balanced tower on the cooker and he's filling the sink so I say, "You don't have to go just yet do you?" before Lauren has a chance but when he smiles at me he also catches her eye and his expression changes.

"I think we'd better skedaddle, but let me do these plates first," and of course I have to insist that he doesn't because he's a guest and Lauren says, very gently, "Listen to her, Mike."

After that Jennifer and Matt say they're too full for dessert but I make them stay for espresso, which takes ages to make and about thirty seconds to drink. And then it's just Stephen, Lee and me and I'm incapable of sitting still because if I do I don't know what we'll say to each other. Lee sits on the sofa finishing the wine that everyone else bought, and Stephen chooses some music, plays two minutes of a song then changes it again, then again, and again until he settles on something frenetic-sounding with a South African beat. I drink G&Ts in the kitchen till it's impossible to not join them because neither of them seem to be leaving. "Do you want anything else to eat? Or drink?" I say. "No you're alright," Lee says. "I'm fine," Stephen says. "Thanks for having us, it was fun." Then he puts on another song and picks up a magazine that I'd tried to tidy away on the bookshelf. Typical that he reaches for that in between the Norton Anthologies I've been lugging round since uni. "Did you have a nice night?" "Of course," I say. Because it would be too awful to admit that I hadn't enjoyed a second of it. "I like Mike," Lee says. "Me too," I say, and I notice Stephen notice this mutual agreement. "I'm pretty tired," he says and as he stands up Lee stands up too, smooths down the rucks in his trousers where his knees have been, but Stephen says, "No no, you stay Lee, it's fine, you finish your drink." Lee looks at his three-quarter-full wine glass as if it might say something to help. "Easy solution – either you both stay or you both leave," I say as a joke, but then I'm not sure how that would be a joke in any way, and it didn't come out relaxed and jokey, it came out more insistent than it should've, and Lee sits back down next to me so fast it was like he was waiting for that, and then he says, "Turn up the music, Stephen," and Stephen obeys.

Blind Spots

Meredith: clean hair, frank face, a dusky blue Fjällräven backpack faded from chasing summer and sudden rain on hills. She's all heavy socks and thin, strong arms. She carries an ancient map, something her dad bought from a supermarket in the nineties that marks every Safeway that isn't there any more. She carries it around like a treasure map, as if it might lead her to something rather than somewhere; the sound of the creases as she opens out the side flaps is enthralling, a journey of long soft moments, rung out. She traces lines of motorways with a long finger and a stubby nail to hear the scratchings of her anticipation. With a ruler it's fourteen-and-three-quarter centimetres from where she started out from to Glasgow.

She adores subways, logical and direct and colour-coded; she pins planners to her wall. Prague, Berlin, London. She tells herself it's because she likes orderly movement, craves evidence of people in such a mass they become a system, lives turned into a kind of fuel. But the subway here is one big loop, which means she'll likely make the same mistakes over and over.

Meredith has a small flat and a crummy job and an email chain in her account about the penalties of withdrawing from a course of study after the fees deadline. Every morning she rides the orange loop to work and thinks about circling, cycling, swirling. The greyish whirlpool of a bath draining, the eddies of a gutter clogged with trash and autumn's rotting leaves. When she finds herself drifting into these thoughts she tries to sit perfectly still and consider the difference between finding and stealing; a self-imposed deadline is looming.

It has become a kind of ritual, counting the stack of cards in open envelopes on top of the dresser every few days, a way to re-establish order through the time frame they present. An initial baffling surprise, turning into a kind of punctuation: they come monthly, sometimes more frequently for special occasions. No postcode; no return address at all. She has almost started to rely on them, which is the great danger. Once this happens, she will have to move on, uproot.

Dear Christina,

Happy Easter. We are thinking of you and wishing for your safety and happiness on this holiday. Your father is better now, and continues to hope for word from you. Elaine is certain his leg will be completely back to normal within six months. That is one of the many things we are grateful for this spring, and hope that you too can share this with us. I enclose a little something that I hope you can use wisely. Please reply, Christina, we only want to know that you are safe and happy.

Dear Christina,

I wonder how close to the 17th this will reach you. I still cannot tell how long it usually takes. Please write and tell me. It's very late and I wonder if I will be able to post this tomorrow. Please let me know when this reaches you, Christina, and try to believe that we only want to know how you are, and to give you our love. I enclose a little something that I hope you can use wisely.

Dear Christina,

Happy Christmas. We love you so much, Christina, and we miss you terribly this year. We want so badly just to know you are safe and happy. Please find some way to give us a sign – please let us know you are alright. I enclose a little something that I hope you can use wisely. Please try to think of me and your father during this holiday.

Dear Christina,

Dear Christina,

Dear Christina,

Dear Christina,

Dearest Christina,

Meredith lasted until the eleventh card before using the money – wisely. The absence of names made it easy at first. Just *Love, your mother. Love, Mum and Dad. Love from your parents. With all our love.* An intensity of feeling combined with a total lack of distinguishing information. The pictures were always completely heart-wrenching – kittens playing with ribbon, a pair of gardening shears on a sun-warmed wooden bench. A charity shop purchase perhaps. The envelopes from Woolworths, forty to a package. Blame is a light thing, she thinks, a thing with little agency. You can wear it, or you can reject it. It is always your own choice. It hasn't got the power to persist; it wanders, rooting around looking for somewhere to rest.

When she left home the first time she did as her father told her and left word of where she was. But there were always other older men with advice that was more suited to her situation, like where the next best sunset was, which train had the fewest ticket inspectors, where to sleep without being moved on. She'd had a place once, where people could find her. But in a fit of pique one day, after a conversation about authentic experiences with a woman called Tahnie who had a tigress tattooed across her torso ("No, it's not a tiger," Tahnie would say, "it's a tigress"), she changed all her numbers and instead passed along messages through old friends which became more garbled and soon failed to reach anyone that mattered. There was a weak link in her game of whispers. Someone who changed 2a to 2b, South to Southwark, Sea to Ocean. At first she imagined the confusion and pain of her mother, and then that dulled, the way a voice is forgotten and can never be recaptured. Salvation lay in resisting attachment, or something like that. She stayed with a boy with a cowlick and a nickname for a while. She liked to untie his bracelets and rest four fingers on the pale patch of revealed wrist. He had a high-tog sleeping bag and a few friends with floors. So they slept on porches, on sofa cushions, cleaned where they could, cooked when they could. But she liked the noise, and he liked the quiet. She liked the traffic, the trappings of travelling with too many people, the chatter and movement. Sometimes she'd ask him to hum till she fell asleep. But this was too wearying, so he left, looked to the mountains for an accompanying quiet while she stuck to the cities.

Meredith used the money for vegetables first. Earthy, dense ones: parsnip, swede, carrot. A mist gathered in the cold flat as she boiled dinner into submission. This was wise. Slowly, she ate her way upwards, opening the cards with a more eager finger. Scrubbed new potatoes, celery hearts, delicate sprouts that she steamed and tossed with finely chopped garlic. One day she swapped butter for a glass bottle of olive oil. From then it was wild mushrooms, vibrant broccoli, a fat heirloom tomato that lasted two days, and then eventually on to a final graduation of avocado, goat's cheese and fresh blueberries that she burst against her palate with a slender finger that she then drew out of her mouth, sucking the purple skins from between her teeth. She stopped short at paper-thin scrolls of smoked meat, and wine, even if it was on offer. But the regularity of the cards suggested these were temporary limits, maybe the final few steps in a prolonged, ill-advised, incredible seduction.

She didn't stop herself at an umbrella from a charity shop one day when she forgot hers at home. And this allowance opened up further opportunities: a pair of red shoes, a thin leather belt, a grey woollen cardigan. Christina's parents, whoever they were, would understand. They'd want – they obviously wanted – the money to help, to be useful. Without identifying information it was easy for them to stay blurry, to see them as not quite real people, unlike her own parents, who were locked into specificity. This was simply a mum and dad, trying to help, trying maybe to make up for something.

Sometimes, when she walked in the city, she imagined Christina. Maybe Christina was the bus driver who took so much verbal abuse from various passengers that Meredith eventually stopped taking the bus, even when it rained. Maybe Christina was the crossing guard who somehow knew the name of every child that trotted towards the school each morning, even behind scarves and hoods and the sameness of uniforms. But she must be younger. Perhaps Christina was the one who stamped out library books or fitted plastic lids on takeaway cappuccinos. But to Meredith this felt like placing the narrowest peg in the widest hole. Maybe Christina was the young woman who stabbed her boyfriend's mother on the same street Meredith lived on, or the mother of the infant who used the stained rickety stroller parked outside the flat below Meredith's. Or she was the Christina who always asked

Meredith to cover her shifts at work, giving her hardly any notice and knowing Meredith would always agree.

Dear Christina,

This afternoon I met your old fourth-year teacher, near the bus stops. I said you were fine. Do you remember him? I enclose a little something that I hope you can use wisely. He sent you his best, as do I. Please call, Christina, I would so love to hear your voice just for a moment.

This most recent card gave Meredith pause. For the past three days she had scrabbled her hand into the bank of cold metal postboxes on the ground floor of her building, reaching and yearning, hungry for it. Her first reaction upon finally feeling the rasping paper was annoyance. *What took you so long?* With all my love, Mum. After she read the note she concluded that this must be it. Time to go. She'd been detaching for a while; the email chain about pending fees was getting longer and longer, gathering links to options for repayment of her student stipend and attachments of her incomplete transcript, and this latest viciousness towards Christina's pathetic parents seemed like the final nail, or the final straw. She recognised this feeling from the past – the internal thud of an ending, crossing over a line or a limit. Time to try again somewhere else.

The morning of a first snow one winter she sat in bed fully dressed with even her trainers on and remembered her mother's boyfriend walking her home from ballet one January, her in her welly boots and tutu, stopping outside a grand house with a grand lawn, untouched by footprints, no marks from birds or animals, just clean and bright, lit with frost. "That's what we should all aspire to," he'd said, and Meredith couldn't resist, had jerked away from him and started running in circles, pushing down hard to make the grass creak beneath her boots. Panting and looking up at his face when she had to stop and catch her breath. He'd given her a look and then announced, "That's a shame," and she knew then that she wouldn't stay, couldn't stay.

Her mother couldn't help herself when Meredith told her where she was moving to; she tutted just as she always had done. Meredith imagines her now, grown even more greyish and peckish and jumpy, quicker to judge and slower to forgive. The time away taught Meredith that people didn't change, maybe couldn't change. *They can't change*, she says to herself, trying to be gentle, remembering all the ways in which she'd done something that was a shame, shameful, in all the years since that snowfall.

The next day she puts her potted plants on the other side of her windowsill, leaving them to fend for themselves. She draws the curtains and uses gaffer tape to seal the slit in the metal postbox assigned to her flat. When she walks over the bridge she drops its corresponding key into the river, even though this will mean losing her deposit. She's learnt by now that she needs these rules, these penalties. The greater her weakness, the more she needs to create boundaries and consequences; her mother taught her that, even though Meredith tried not to absorb the lesson. In her backpack are a grey woollen cardigan, a thin leather belt and a pair of red shoes, things to keep her warm, gifts from Christina's mum and dad that she knows she truly deserves.

On the train that's headed south she folds out the map again, lets her finger and thumb pirouette east and west this time, towards a place where the red lines of major roads gather into a clot, with enough Safeways for supplies.

Wednesdays

On Tuesdays Dani's ex has her kid overnight so on Wednesdays she needs us. Even more of a low talker, she finds ways to get close. She wants to see what you're photocopying, who you're emailing; she touches your shoulder to check if you're on the phone instead of doing the thumb-and-pinkie hand-wiggle like everyone else. Monica says Wednesdays are a good time to dig in the blade. Dani's my boss and I've gotten both my raises on a Wednesday. Plus the time I had to take a week off right before budget because my flatmate moved out without really telling me, that was on a Wednesday too. Monica says she can smell it, low defences and a desire to people-please; sometimes I think I can too. It's like dairy products, or maybe hair dye?

Monica sits across from me and clacks her tongue stud along her bottom row of teeth because she likes to let people know she's alternative. Monica makes her own Caesar salad dressing at home (1 clove garlic, 2 anchovies, a loose handful of grated Parmesan, 5 tbsp mayonnaise, 1 tbsp white wine vinegar), and when she eats at her desk the smell pours out of her Tupperware till Dani says it's flooding the whole office, tumbling all the way over on to our side of the room. I see the fake panic of deadlines on her face on spacious afternoons when Dave says we're all fucking the dog but stuck till five. Dani's easily distracted and by almost anything. She sits side-on to the window, whorling her hair round a biro and looking at nothing, especially not the view. Sometimes I pretend to be, I want to say wistful? But I think I need to practise in the mirror because one day Dave said did I need something extra to do because I looked bored. Dani said that was uncalled for and he didn't have any right and Monica said Dave's a dick not your manager and at lunchtime Dani brought in treats. I'm not daft. I know that if the cleaner moves the bin when she's hoovering to make sure it goes back next to the temp's desk because being by the trash is bad.

I like to get in early; it means I can leave early, even though I mostly don't, depends how people are, what kind of meetings Dani's had and does she want to talk about it. I can get a coffee from the free dispenser in the kitchen that no one uses but me, and some people in Finance I guess, because Dave says it tastes like frothy come and Monica thought that was hilarious and said, "Oh my god! You're actually totally right!" and there's a Starbucks just across the street anyway. But I think it tastes fine. If I'm really early and there's definitely no one about I always feel this compulsion to take off my shoes and sit in the other chairs, an urge which I try to control after the time Dave caught me spinning behind Monica's desk and I had to use up one of the good excuses to distract him, and now I can't remember which one and I'm scared I'll say it again. I think maybe it was about checking to see if she'd left her charger because my phone was flat? Dave's the worst, I think. But when I told everyone he looked weedy in his new glasses no one said anything and maybe they just weren't paying attention or maybe they all agreed and so didn't answer, but maybe the silence was a bad sign. Everyone knows you shouldn't be the last one to say something in a conversation, because if it just hangs there dangling like a hand towel on a washing line that you've forgotten to bring in, it means no one cares and that's not the goal.

Sometimes I pretend not to hear when Dani says *Do you want a brew?* or *Did you have a good weekend?* because then it seems like you've got other things on your mind and it lets everyone know that they come second, or maybe even third. *I can't talk to you right now, my life outside of work that you don't get to see is big and wild and you don't know one single ounce of it and that makes me mysterious.* I read on Buzzfeed that "treat 'em mean keep 'em keen" is how you should handle your office relationships as well as your boyfriends.

Dani strides past our desk cluster and drops a stack of paper on her keyboard. "Good thing I did a degree in *childcare!*" she says over her shoulder in a whisper-shout, so that we can hear but no one outside our area can. Dave snorts and Monica goes "mm-*hmmm*" and normally I'm the one that snorts so after a bit I say, "Welcome to the monkey house!" but I've left it, damn, I've left it too long and Monica gives Dave a look. Then she unfurls from her desk – she always kicks off her shoes and sits cross-legged in her chair, even in summer when anyone can see the dirty bottoms of her feet if they walk by – and stands up, shaking out her loose genie pants.

"Are you coming out this afternoon? The thought of frozen margaritas is the only thing getting me through right now."

"Maybe. I have to meet some people later on, but I guess I could come for one," says Dave.

I know that I like frozen margaritas because I went to a Mexican restaurant once and the waiter said if I was too full for dessert I should try one of those instead. *Like an alcoholic slush puppy,* he said. And I laughed and he laughed so I tipped him ten quid and had to take the bus home from the stop behind the church because I didn't have any more cash to get into a cab with the rest of them, and the other bus stop is too close to the taxi stand.

"Absolutely," Dani's leaning against the door of her office, "a margarita is pretty much the only thing that will keep me from killing you-know-who right now."

"Oh, I know who."

"If people would just *listen* before ordering a committee meeting, which will do nothing and—"

"We'll make yours a double then, shall we?" I put in, and

Dani gives me a real laugh and I have to get up and go to the bathroom before my face turns red.

Once when Monica was checking Facebook, which she always does at the end of the day, she said, "Oh jeez, look, Urban Outfitters are selling Walkmans," and I said, "I already have one," without thinking, and she looked at me for so long and just wouldn't turn away. I could feel it somehow, even though I was staring at my computer screen, like the way you can tell when a TV is on even when you're in another room. And I thought about it for a long time afterwards but I couldn't come to any kind of useful conclusion. I still have all my cassettes and I don't plan on getting rid of them. My Walkman still works great. I suppose I could have shown it to Monica but I didn't even think of that until later.

When someone has a birthday they get to choose where we all go out to celebrate, and Dave is normally the one who puts it into everyone's calendar. Dani's birthday isn't till tomorrow but these drinks tonight aren't in my calendar, and I'm starting to panic about it. Dani made fun of him the first time he did it but she's always first to reply to the meeting invite, and anyway everyone puts everything in their calendars. Monica even puts her counselling appointments in there. For a while Dani had weekly mediation appointments with her ex, and she put those in there too: Miriam Greenbaum, Family Mediation, 32 Trenton Avenue, 2–3 p.m. One time I put "Gynaecologist" in at 12 p.m. to see if anyone would notice, but no one said anything about it, and when the fifteen-minute warning window popped up I picked up my things and left, or else people would think I was missing my appointment. I just went down the road and flicked through the sales rack at Zara for forty-five minutes and came back; I wasn't sure how long that kind of thing should really take. I've bought Dani a card in case it's an oversight and

I did think about just putting it in my own calendar, but without Dave doing it I thought it'd look desperate.

By 5:03 everyone's just about left the office without really saying anything but then Dave sticks his head round the door and says, "Come on slowpoke we're all waiting for you," and I basically lose it, scrabble around for all my shit like they might leave without me at any moment, and forget her card in my desk drawer like an idiot. Had my Bobbi Brown lipstick in my bag though, just in case.

It's two-for-one from five till seven so we order doubles every twenty minutes to make sure we're stockpiled but actually everyone just drinks them faster because they're in front of us and the waitress knows to make the most of us. Dave's sleeves are rolled up now and the tiled table has left little indentations on his elbows like the elastic line of a sock round an ankle. He keeps scratching at it with his short nails and even though there's music I can hear his skin sounds dry. Trying to keep track of what people are saying is tough because they start something as a group, taking it in turns and letting the topic move between them but then someone just has to get off whatever's on their chest and their rant is on top of another person's point and they split off for a second with a partner and I'm trying to hear what seems most important but the noise is tough to chew through so all I catch are the occasional scowls, the closed-eye serious shakes of a head or a quick glance, mouth open, at the exit.

Finally Dani says to me, "Did you hear Ashleigh was attacked in the front office? Some guy came in and verbally abused her."

"Oh my god I cover reception sometimes. I'm so glad it wasn't me."

Dani looks at me, not for long because she gets distracted but it was there, her half-glare like she's checking a cashier is giving her the right change. I don't make eye contact with her again because I know I've said something I shouldn't have although I'm not totally sure what, so instead I focus on Monica, who's describing to Dave something about her new email signature. If her title's changed, I need to know that. Eventually I realise that's not what she's talking about at all, it's something about corporate credit cards, but by this point it's too hard to keep the information straight so I decide to leave, say I'm meeting someone and that they're going to walk me home. But I can't find the waitress who hung up our coats and it looks like there's been a shift change because I can't see her anywhere, so I try to approach the bar.

I ask a woman with a silver ring through the middle bit of her nose, "Can I have my coat? It's a Burberry rain jacket."

"I don't have it sweetie, you'll have to ask your server." She's not paying attention to me in the slightest, she might as well be talking to someone somewhere under the bar, and she seems entirely unconcerned about the jacket.

"She's not here any more, could you look for it please?"

"I'm in the middle of something darling," she's topping up a fourth pint with one hand and holding an empty glass at an angle with the other, ready to move it under the tap and make a fifth, "I'll ask someone to attend to you."

I want to leave quick in case one of them walks past on their way to the bathroom and we have to say goodbye again. I think I did a good job with the first one and I don't want to ruin it by getting it wrong the second time.

"I just want my coat, where are they kept?"

"I'm afraid only staff are allowed in the cloakroom."

"Look it's a Burberry jacket, it's expensive, could you please just go get it for me."

"I will, as soon as I finish these drinks," she says almost sing-songy, like you do with a child who's about to lose it, or maybe when you're about to lose it. I'm not actually sure how this stuff goes with children. Then she starts mixing a vodka-soda.

"Don't start serving someone else, I'm asking you to get my coat."

She's doing something, turning her head away from me and looking down the bar to where the barbacks are twisting tea towels into ropes to wipe away the smudges of lipstick from rims. She's making a face or mouthing something.

"Hey, excuse me," I say, "look at me. I think you just need to do your job, do as I'm telling you, and just get my coat."

"You'll need to put that back," she says sharply. I've taken one of her pints because that's the only thing she'll pay attention to. Some has slopped over the rim of the glass and it's running between my fingers. She turns to wave to someone, and I drink some, because I'm not sure what else to do. That Burberry jacket was a find; I spent hours in the Oxfam next to work on lunch breaks when everyone else was going for sushi and I don't know how to use wasabi and it was just easier to say I was busy. But it all paid off one day, great condition, no busted seams, fourteen quid, my size. Normally it's such a rip-off; half the time they have saggy faded Primark polyester for the same price it would've been new like we don't know that they cut the tags out of the cheapest stuff.

Then Dave is there all of a sudden and he takes the pint out of my hand. Those indents are still on his elbows and his forearm flesh is kind of doughy, a little damp and pinkish.

"This cunt won't do her job!" I say to him, and he shrugs his shoulders and puts his other palm up, like he's saying *it wasn't me*, and then it's creeping up inside me, the knowledge that I've ruined Dani's birthday, rising up along with the taste of bad beer and two measly tacos without any sour cream because it was too far down the table and I didn't want to ask.

"Come on," he says, "time to go eh?" and he's kind of grinning at how behind the bar security staff have gathered and the bartender whose pint I've stolen is saying something to a tall guy wearing a black coat and an earpiece.

There's this energy brewing as she points at us and I start grinning too: "Come on, let's get out of here!"

He rides in the taxi with me because it turns out he lives quite close and I'd only agreed because it meant splitting the fare but then he paid it all anyway so I thought it'd be rude not to invite him up. He's standing looking at all the stuff on my shelves while I make coffee. I remember someone saying once you should never make instant for guests if you can help it but I'm kind of wired from calling the girl at the bar a cunt and then flagging a taxi like it was a getaway car, so I stir up some Nescafé and then just hold the cup to get the blood out of my ears and into my hands. Anyway, I can't help it, I haven't got any other kind.

"Are these tapes?" he asks as I hand him his. "Bit out of date aren't they? What have you got these all for then?"

And because I'm thinking about the coat and the cunt I say, "I just like them. I like the neat way they all stack up, I don't want to throw them away," which as soon as I've said it I know sounds weird, or at least dull, in any case all wrong, like trying to play a triangle while you're still holding it.

But all Dave says is "huh". Then, "I kept my records for years. Got rid of them all recently. I heard it's cool again. Could've sold them and made a buck. It's much better to have a thing in your hands, right?" And I nod.

He drinks his coffee and then he goes because Dave isn't really my type, he's maybe fifteen years older than me and although I know what coming up meant I figure the mystery is better. They'll all know that we left together. I know that at work in the morning they'll all be muttering and they'll love playing me up, saying *good night was it?* and I'll say *yes thanks* and they'll say *you look tired* and I'll say *went to bed late* and nothing else. I know I'll get the words just right because I'll be thinking about it all night, exactly how to fix my face, when to arrive (maybe 9:04, just a little bit later than normal), and it'll be worth feeling knackered to get up at 5:30 and get my hair all tousled and smoke up my eyeliner a wee bit so they aren't quite sure what kind of night I've had but I still look really good. I lie awake thinking about it, wondering if it's a bit too far to give myself a hickey, I can sort of get my own collarbone, or at least around there, and you can also do it with two fingers, it's way harder but I've figured out how. I decide not to though because it's no good if people know you've done the thing you're hinting at, even if you haven't.

I get in at 9:17, which, okay, is stretching it, but the later bus I took was later than it was actually supposed to be, and five past is one thing, but quarter past is really another, and this cuts way too close to our Thursday morning 9:30 meeting. I'm sweating from running up the hill to try and make up the time and right away I can tell something is off. Dani looks up at me when I get in but then immediately looks down again, almost like she's pretending she didn't see me in the first place. Monica is drinking her almond milk coffee and when I sit in my seat it feels warm.

In the 9:30 meeting Dani says in front of everyone that it's her birthday so she's taking the afternoon off and actually come to think of it she'll just go after this meeting. That's pretty much the end of it because Dave and Monica have no feedback regarding the week's initiatives and when Dani turns to me I just shrug and rub my eyes, and then I remember about my eye make-up and freeze, lifting my balled fists away from my eyes slowly like I've touched wet paint and I might be able to leave most of it intact. After Dani leaves it's awful; mid-morning on a Thursday and no one's saying anything and I can still feel last night's Nescafé mixing with the cocktails, churning under the bits of toast I had this morning when I was waiting around to leave late. I try to think of something else, softball or deadbolts or passport renewal forms, but it doesn't help. Then Dave sends me a calendar invite for a date – dinner on Friday – and I have to go to the bathroom, the downstairs one for disabled people, of which there are none in our office just now, and which I happen to know Dani used to use to pump breast milk, because she'd keep it in a little metal bottle in the fridge and she'd go in and out of the bathroom with a little pink cloth bag with all the parts in there, and one day she came out of a meeting that ran over and had a wet patch over one breast as she scurried for the door. The disabled toilet is further away from our workspace but the walls are thin and there's a hole for a big bunch of wires to come in through the cavity and up into the ceiling and I can hear someone on the phone in the basement office so I figure they must be able to hear me so I lay loo roll in layers across the water to try and muffle the sounds but it doesn't make a difference, I can't clench it quiet or keep it in, the whole night comes pouring out of me. I close my eyes and wait for it to be over; the hand soap I pour into the bowl to try and mask the smell does nothing but foam.

When I come back to our office space only Monica is sitting there, cross-legged and picking slender carrot sticks out of her Tupperware. She watches me sit down and I'm worried she's noticed I was away for longer than a pee would take but that's not it at all; she waits until I'm about to unlock my screen and then she tells me that she's been fucking Dave since the week before our last quarterly.

"I haven't told anyone about it. So nobody else knows. But I think you ought to know."

She says it light and casual, like all the times she's told me the sandwich of the day in the shop downstairs, and I know this is it, this is important and that a key is turning. I'll explain to her that it's all a mistake, that he just took me home and didn't even make a move and then she'll apologise and mention another thing or two and I'll laugh, and then she'll say even more stuff, spilling all the details about their office hook-ups, how he can't keep his hands off her and how when they're alone in the kitchen she lets him get away with everything. Now we'll be friends, because I listen to everything so closely and she'll appreciate me. And when

I have dinner with Dave it'll be fine, because Monica and I will have talked all about it, and I can hear more about his records, and maybe he'll play me one if he kept any, one that he just couldn't bear to part with. We'll sit on his bedroom floor, and it'll be her we talk about and I'll hear about how daft she is when they're alone. This is how she wants it to be, I'm sure, but she's playing it cool and I can too. The three of us will be solid, and then back at the office, when Dani speaks or asks a question it'll be me that stares, shocked that she really has no idea about anything.

"Oh. Okay," I say, and click "accept" on Dave's invite. "That's nice."

The Letting Out

The web page lists all the equipment required, with a scrollable list of its top three tips for a successful experience. The second top tip is "take the garment off if possible". The third is "use a mirror". Alison wonders what kind of button-sewing situations might make it impossible to take clothes off, and how surely it's harder to thread a needle looking in a mirror. She puts her phone on the counter, folds her trousers over the heated towel rail, sits on the toilet and throws the popped button into the bin, which makes a gong-like crash from the rebound off its metal lip. It isn't the button's fault. The trousers are old. She bought them maybe seven years ago with Christmas money from one of her aunties, she can't remember which one, and they'd lasted really well. The first time she washed them they'd dyed a white bra a bland puce like an unwashed tongue. But they were such a good length, just skimming her ankles, and they'd worn really politely at the knees, turning lightly into lacy threads, so she'd kept them and washed them separately each and every time she wore them.

If she was her mother's daughter she'd have a sewing kit from a hotel in her bag. But she's never stayed in a hotel that provides that kind of thing; most of them didn't even have a kettle. After thinking about it too much she realises there was actually only that one place with a kettle, miniature like one from a doll's house or something, which throws into relief all the other places she's stayed at without this one, basic implement. Not that she's been that many places, and the doll's kettle was in that place she and her cousin Mona had stayed at for Sandy Lowell's destination wedding, and it took them half an hour to make two cups of tea because you could only do one at a time and it kept turning off before it boiled. Do other people get caught up in this kind of thing, she wonders, tripping down connected memories, by themselves and in secret? Like smelling yourself or not always washing your hands when you should? Sandy had gone to bed earliest after downing a shocking number of drinks and saying wetly into Mona's ear on her way back to the room that her feet were so cold they were about to freeze right off and wouldn't that be a nice distraction from all this shit. Mona'd told Sandy she swore to god she'd keep this secret but Sandy had looked at her completely baffled. Cousin Mona who'd just turned eighteen and who didn't get out very much, according to Alison's mum. Cousin Mona with the good genes, the good skin and teeth.

The button had burst about sixteen hours ago. "Don't be like that," he'd said. "I can't help it," he'd said, "you know I can't help it." In the sixteen hours since, she's had four cans of beer, a snack-size crinkly bag of cheese and onion crisps, a crusty swipe of drying hummus off the side of a glass serving bowl that had been left out, two painkillers and a flowery glass of rosé.

Paul lives across town, in a poky flat above the herbal medicine shop where she once bought some dusty nettle tea after reading an online article about rapid weight loss, but he wasn't living there then. The first time they went to his place Alison told him the nettle tea story and he gripped the fat above her hip and said, "Guess it didn't work, then," but laughed, to show he didn't mind the extra space she continued to take up.

The top of Paul's tongue is oddly smooth, almost lacking in texture, so that sometimes she can't shake the sensation of a slick latex glove, or some kind of flat wet balloon, gliding across her nipple. It's something she has an urge to chew on to really understand, like a teething baby. She tried to slow him down the first few times, surprised and curious about this new sensation, but he batted her hand away and then the second time looked her in the eye when he did it, so she gave up and figured some people were just like that.

Paul had met her out for drinks after work one day, stopping her on the way to the bathroom with enough certainty that initially she thought he was mistaking her for someone he knew. When she realised he hadn't she figured she was meant to be flattered, which at first she was. He took her phone number from her and that was it, he was off. She needed the bathroom so badly she was practically dancing, and finally he let her go, tucking his phone back into his jeans and heading back to his mates. He didn't look her way once for the rest of the evening, but when she got home, there was a text already.

Alison taps at her phone and goes to call her mum but the music in the living room has gone quiet so she sends a text instead: "Evening going great ;) will be back late xxx." She hears the tick-tick-tick of the needle jumping, a familiar sound even though she's never owned a record player. He's been playing something she doesn't know; seventies sounding, just a bassline going round and round until some tinny synthesiser prompts a key change and the whole thing starts again and then again, for fifteen straight minutes. She wanted to listen to *Abba Greatest Hits*, something he has two copies of despite insisting that neither are his.

"Paul? Paul!"

He must be on the balcony smoking. Her phone pings:

"Good :) ive left some cheese pie on the table working early so dont wake me up when you come in." Her mum usually likes to hear about everything that's happened on a date, to get all the details. She'll be asleep with the TV flashing light around her room, on mute so she can drift off, but needing the company, the subtitles scrolling up the screen. And even if Alison doesn't have anything much to say she likes saying goodnight, maybe even getting into bed for a bit and watching the last twenty minutes of whatever late-night chat show is still on while her mum gets a glass of water and settles herself again. Alison's mouth fills with saliva at the thought of cheese pie and she stretches her arms up, easing her ribs away from her stomach, giving herself some breathing space.

She hears the balcony door slide shut along its dusty track and the music start again abruptly in the middle of a song with a different monotonous bassline. Paul's flat is never totally clean; it's her umpteenth time here, and she's developed the feeling that each time she comes over he's focused on just one thing – wiping the sink or the bathroom mirror, putting all his clothes in the closet – and ignoring everything else until the cycle starts over. She looks at herself in the toothpaste-stained mirror, wondering if she can bear putting the trousers back on. If she can get the fly to lie flat once it's zipped up, it almost doesn't need a button. She hears him walk around the living room a little bit, recognising the clink of glass on glass, and then his footsteps get closer. She silently reaches over to unflick the bathroom door lock. He won't like that. She opens it for him a little bit when she hears him pause.

He sticks his hand in first, a meaty paw smothering a bottle of beer. She takes the bottle, then he puts his head around the door.

He frowns. "Just get a new pair."

"I don't want a new pair."

"I'll get you a new pair."

"I won't wear them," she says without thinking.

His frown doesn't budge, and he narrows his eyes slightly. He sniffs theatrically. One nostril is partially blocked from a cold that has clung on for longer than she likes, so that he's still periodically making sounds like a frustrated animal. He's been off work for a week and felt sorry enough for himself to keep her away. He said he didn't want to make her ill, but she knows that's not really it. He's wrong. Of course she can take care of him. She knows how to keep a person hydrated. Either way, his sense of humour hasn't taken a hit.

"I smell it."

"Paul. Just give me a minute."

"I smell bullshit. It fucking stinks."

He snorts again, sucking up all the air in the bathroom, sucking the air from her lungs even, till she gets light-headed and wonders how she'll ever get the energy to stand up. He has a green speck of grocery-store guacamole in the thick hair of his sideburns, a tiny dot the size of a sesame seed, but it's stark against the golden red of his hair. Suddenly he smacks the door on its outside, bashing it with the flat of his palm. She jumps so high that she spills a little beer froth down her knee.

"Do you smell that?"

"Paul, please fuck off for just five minutes."

"We're going to implement an elastic-only rule. Stretchy pants or skirt. That's it. Wear a skirt next time. That's clever. Do that."

When her mum saw the state of her favourite purple jeans she went straight to the sewing tin on her dressing table, suggesting a couple of blue denim patches for the knees, saying, "They'll look cool, you know, kind of seventies," and showing her where she could sew the button back on to give her a little more room. But by the time she was done they draped strangely, the fly becoming a bulging ridge when she sat down, as if she had a mushy dick lolling about under there, and the patches made her look like a children's TV presenter. Her mum insisted they looked great with such exuberant conviction that Alison drew her eyebrows together and folded the jeans up methodically. She decided to go in a different direction.

"Can I borrow this? And maybe your boots too?"

Her mum has kept a suede skirt and leather knee-highs from the eighties that she still wears sometimes, like when she meets old friends for drinks. She keeps them wrapped in plastic in her wardrobe.

"Okay but they need a polish."

Alison steps into the skirt but can't pull the zip.

"It's a bit tight at the waist."

"Well your leggings are too thick probably," her mum says quickly. "There's no give in suede," a statement Alison doesn't need to hear.

The boots, on the other hand, have little triangles of stretchy elastic at their tops which sit snug against her calves. She puts a long angora sweater on over just her bra and thinks she looks quite good in the full-length mirror on the door of her mum's wardrobe.

"Are you going somewhere?"

"Maybe."

She thinks about the fluff from her top sticking to Paul's tongue and lips, sitting like snow in his eyelashes, and feels sweat start to pool on her upper lip.

"Are you feeling okay? You've gone a bit red. Have you eaten enough today?" She hasn't and she can't hide it. "I'll make you something. A cheese sandwich – something light. You need to keep your blood sugar up."

"Not sure how much cheese helps blood sugar," Alison murmurs, swallowing involuntarily.

Her mother scoffs, "Don't be silly, a young healthy girl like you, you need your energy."

They both go downstairs, Alison heading to the fridge for the butter almost instinctively.

Her mum has already gone to the cooker to turn the heat on under a pan. "Lucky guy," she muses awkwardly, trying hard not to make it a question.

Her mum never asks, never pushes. Always wants, though. Always offers. Sometimes Alison feels badly for how much she wants to talk, to be around her mum, how much she wants nothing more than crisp, fried cheese sandwiches and to talk over the outfits of whoever's on the telly, and then she feels even worse for overcompensating by pushing away, deliberately misunderstanding things and closing things down.

"Lucky me, maybe."

"Lucky him," she says firmly. She pauses. Then, "Whoever he is." Then another pause, during which Alison peels back the wrapper of the butter slowly and delicately, so it doesn't tear and so she won't have to lick her fingers clean.

Paul's feeling grumpy. He's been told off by his manager again, who is apparently a total cock who knows nothing, and he's been explaining to Alison the many ways he's been treated unjustly. She lies on the couch with her knees up, flattening a Ferrero Rocher wrapper into a wavering golden square. Her mum won a box in a raffle and suggested she take them, so she's brought them round in an attempt to only eat half. But it hasn't worked.

"You're not listening," he accuses.

"Mmm, of course I am."

He swipes the wrapper out of her hands and crumples it.

"No you aren't."

"He said you should have printed out extra copies and you said the schedule was already stuck up on the door and it was in the second email you sent round and he said, 'Oh well that's a shame but never mind,' because he's a passive aggressive wanker."

"Yeah but that wasn't my point. You totally missed the point."

"I was working on that wrapper. I was going to make it the most beautiful wrapper in this flat."

"Well you fucking aren't any more, are you."

Later he goes down on her for as long as she can stand it, three minutes maybe, because his angle keeps his sharp chin knocking up against her pubic bone and his beard scratching her skin until she taps him on his shoulders and says, "Now me, my turn," just to make it stop.

When she gets home her mum's on the sofa, telly on, sound up. She isn't even in her pyjamas.

"How was your night?"

"Good thanks. What are you watching?"

"Just the news."

She recognises the banner scrolling across the bottom of the screen and wonders why anyone stays up late to watch local news.

"It's nearly midnight."

"I got distracted."

"Did someone cook another giant pancake? Has another kitten been rescued?" Even Alison knows that local news full of bullshit stories is made to make people feel proud and yet also somehow really paranoid. Alison knows she isn't savvy, like street savvy, but she knows she has smarts. She's worked with lots of different kinds of people, she knows how to read them, knows she could either mess around with her mum right now or give her what she wants. "I'm feeling a bit hungry actually, I... missed dinner."

"I can make you something."

"No it's okay. It's late."

"I don't mind, I'm up, not learning anything here."

"Well okay."

They both move into the kitchen and her mum cracks eggs and milk into some Tupperware to microwave.

"So why are you still awake? S'pretty late for you."

"Well actually I phoned your father."

"Why?" Alison nearly shouts this, drowning out the hum of the microwave so that when it pings and the room is quiet again, full of night-time nothingness, the garden pitch-black through the windows, just the small strip of light from under the crockery cupboard downlighting the surfaces, she says it again, "Why," but quieter this time.

"He wasn't in."

"But why did you phone him in the first place?"

"Because he's your father."

"Well sure when he wants to be. Which is almost never."

"He's got a right to know about your life, he'd be proud to hear about you and everything you do."

"I don't do anything. There's nothing to tell him."

"You know that's not true. You've got a good job, you go out on dates, have boyfriends. He'd want to know all that."

"If he truly did he would ask me. Anyway, I've been on *some* dates and Paul is not my boyfriend, we're just seeing each other. We just see each other sometimes."

"Oh, okay. But still."

Alison eats the scrambled eggs straight from the Tupperware. Her mum kisses her on the forehead and goes to bed.

In the morning her mum is up early, has already been to the shops to buy fresh cranberry juice. "It's good for you. Good for your waterworks."

Alison rolls her eyes but pours a large glass, one for each of them. Her mum picks through the local newspaper, lingers on a story about a woman's prizewinning azaleas. She has on her blue dressing gown that she's worn every morning probably for her entire life, the one she was wearing one morning when Sandy Lowell had come to pick Alison up for the walk to school and Alison hadn't managed to get to the door first and had been so embarrassed she hadn't talked to her mum for hours after coming home from school. "For goodness' sake, what do you think Sandy's mum wears around the house?" her mum had asked, remorseful but also infuriatingly mirthful. The memory is nearly a decade old but it sweeps over her so suddenly she speaks up.

"Can you stop phoning Dad please? It's not like he's coming back."

"Of course not darling. He will never stop being your father, though."

"I mean, he's never coming back to you."

Her mother looks up, her finger keeping her place on the newsprint. Alison holds her gaze coolly while she empties the contents of her glass in one go, trying with all her might not to wipe the drip that has escaped down her chin.

That night she goes to Paul's again. He opens the door with a beer in one hand, a bowl in the other and a bottle of soy sauce between his face and shoulder, like a telephone.

"Leftovers. Unless you brought something."

Alison has a paper tray of date squares, half off because of the use-by date, but he agrees that won't do for dinner. She walks into the kitchen and puts the tray on the counter, yelping when he whips her butt with a dishcloth.

"Nicely done – didn't take you long to learn," he says, indicating something about her legs.

She looks down, then realises – her leggings, the saggy ones that aren't so saggy any more. Everything else had felt frumpy or itchy or just not right, so she'd rolled these on, annoyed at how grateful she was to have held on to them through multiple purges.

His leftovers means yesterday's takeaway; he opens white cartons and lets them slop into saucepans, pouring extra soy sauce on everything.

"I'm not sure you're supposed to reheat this, you know."

"It'll be fine."

"You could eat it cold instead," she says, scooping the

corner of a date square with her fingers and popping it into her mouth with her head tilting back.

He puts his hand to her throat, holding her in place: "But I don't want to eat it cold," he says and kisses the dint at the top of her chest. She feels his teeth on her skin, and when she tries to shift she feels the current running through his hands. She swallows, and the lump of oats passes under his stony fingers. It's fine, it has always been fine, from their first date when he'd said to her, "Let's go in one of the booths," so he could sit close enough to be touching her the entire time (she'd chosen a table that had more space for them to spread out but he'd asked her to move), to now. The spaces she can see herself occupying in his life are slowly coming into focus, sharper each time she sees him. She's learning what he likes, what he expects, what openings he's making for her and how to fit into them properly.

When she goes to the bathroom she takes a dry wipe from her bag normally reserved for the pair of glasses she wears at work and rubs away all the toothpaste spots on the bathroom mirror. That night she pretends to fall asleep afterwards, taking slow, deep breaths, and even though he nudges her once or twice he's too lazy to do anything purposefully after he's come so he flops on his back, sighs and is soon snoring. She pokes him a few times to try and get him to roll over in his sleep, but it doesn't work. Eventually she drifts off too but she wakes early, makes a pot of coffee for him and slams his front door hard to make sure he wakes up and realises how thoughtful she's been, how easy it is, inconsequential even, to let her stay over.

On Saturday she meets her mum for lunch at an Italian deli in town. It has become a standing arrangement; every few weeks they do this, and something about the formality of place settings and waitstaff means their chatter takes on a different, more conspiratorial tone. They settle things, agree on things. Her mum texts that she's running late, so Alison takes an extra ten minutes to walk the length of the deli's glass cabinets several times, appraising the meats and cheeses, lingering over stodgy pasta bakes but letting her choice of pastry dictate what she'll actually have for lunch. When her mum finally arrives she's wearing the purple jeans. She's taken the denim patches off and sewn some kind of black material under the knees, emphasising the wisps and threads where the jeans have worn, delicate and pink. They hug her hips in a way that Alison knows means the button has been resewn too. The knee-high boots finish off a look that makes Alison feel more embarrassed than the blue dressing gown ever did.

"Sorry I'm late I just couldn't get parked," she says, and when she catches Alison staring at the jeans, "You don't mind do you? I took them out of the pile for the clothes bank and just, well, had a little fun with them. You know how I like a project."

"I don't mind, they look nice. On you."

"They're yours back anytime you want," she says, half-convincingly.

They eat at a small table tucked behind a concrete column, next to a window that lets in a draught. Every time her mum crosses or uncrosses her legs her leather boots let out a little sigh. She doesn't order a pastry with her coffee but insists that Alison should, and of course she does, chewing mouthfuls of fudgy eclair with her head lowered while her mum sips a tiny espresso.

"I thought I might bring home a takeaway tonight, stay in?" she suggests lightly.

"Bring home from where?"

"I'm getting my hair cut after this, didn't I mention? And then I thought I'd poke around the shops."

"Oh. Well I won't be in tonight."

"Ah. I won't bother. That's fine."

Alison picks up the last few crumbs with a wet fingertip, twirling the plate to make sure she catches every last one.

At Paul's that night all she can think about is the takeaway. About how her mum prefers a place that does an amazing butter chicken, and how she always orders an extra naan. Plus it's Saturday; there's always something good-awful on TV, and biscuits and tea once they've finished dinner.

"Pay attention," Paul mutters.

"I am," she sighs, and then reaches down to help with the last two buttons on her shirt. He smacks her hand away and yanks at the fabric, making it tear, one button lurching out like an eyeball.

"Aha," he says.

Knit

She's never broken a bone, although she'd say she's been close. But by that she means nearby, within sight when people have slipped, tripped and spilt. Within sight, not within the boundaries of her own body. The first was a boy named Gerald, whom she was in love with when she was seven. He wore very clean trainers to school and his brother's glasses precarious on his small nose because he thought it made him look smart till he ruined his sight and he had to get his own pair – much thicker lenses, but a better fit across his face. He'd slipped on wet leaves in the playground and snapped his clavicle, which was a word she thought sounded musical, like the wheeze of an accordion or the ting of the triangle, which was always the instrument she was given to play in Music Hour, though she felt she deserved something more complicated. They'd carried him off on a big flat board, with Mrs Howard the head teacher using her long arms to keep all the children back while two paramedics lifted him gently.

"I'm fine, I'm fine," he kept repeating, humiliated into repetition by the stares and the sniggers and the obvious truth that he'd fallen down over nothing, over his own fragility. She'd started a breaktime sweeping club after that, to round up all the mulch, pressing it into the sides of the school wall until watery brown ran off into the sewers. Gerald came back after four days with a white sling around one arm and the information that he wasn't to strain himself for four to six weeks. She'd caught him up on the logistics of the sweeping club, although winter was coming and no more leaves were really falling. He'd tried to show his appreciation with a firm hug that at first seemed sincere but after a moment or so too long she knew somehow it wasn't right and ran to find someone to tell on him to.

Gerald moved to San Francisco before school ended, tugged along by a parent's high-profile job, which he spoke of in tones dripping with disgust. He hated leaving, feared a place he'd never been. He complained to Steve about it in lunch periods and Steve chewed thoughtfully. Steve's mum didn't have a job. Gerald left on a Thursday and on the Friday Steve tripped walking home and sprained his ankle so badly that after a week his father finally drove him to the hospital to discover the talus was snapped and in the car home he kept saying, "I'm sorry, son… I'm so sorry," and Steve couldn't ever untangle all these events in the coming years, even though he never heard from Gerald again. The ankle twinged forever more, and it always brought him back to school, the terrifying whims of teachers and the sinister silence of the hallways when you've been called down to the office.

The first time Steve ever saw the ocean it was on a trip to Atlantic City for a high-school buddy's stag. It was warm and frothy with a film on top, like a cheap coffee from the place in the lobby of the office building he temped in, and he didn't think it was particularly beautiful but he knew it had to mean something, or at least it should, to make this worth the time off and the cost of the trip. He took deep breaths, his nostrils aimed at the cresting waves. The stag, James, got his nose broken that first night by his best man when, at the craps table, he put the two dice in his mouth for luck. The punch to the face propelled the dice down the table to score double fours and win the game. Is what the best man said at the wedding. In reality, James got kicked out a little too roughly and spent the rest of the early morning hours in a sports bar telling everyone who would listen what a great girlfriend he had and how she definitely wouldn't care about the wedding photos.

Standing in the corner of the office in City Hall where his daughter was getting married to her partner after years of nagging from the kids, James was reminded of his own wedding and how completely different it was. His was all soft confetti, dainty lace gloves that felt dusty in his hands. Nothing like today. The creases in Martha's pantsuit were so sharp and the tie she'd given him to wear was straight with a small, tight knot. Martha (named after James's mum) was forty-six and James was pushing eighty but still did four limping laps around the track at the Y every morning, one new hip and one old one making figure eights to the thudding beats of youth basketball below. Martha's twins, stiff in formal shirts and creased pants, flopped around on the plastic chairs, half bored and half thrilled at all the activity and strangers. It was Martha's birthday, too, *chosen so that he'd have one less date to remember*, her goofy partner hu-yucked to anyone who'd listen. Either by accident or design, the ceremony was scheduled for just a few minutes after the time she'd burst into the world, in a gush of blood and god knows what else, a roaring from up above as his wife tried to get off the ride and couldn't. The delivery broke her tailbone, which Martha Senior made sure to point out to people was an actual break, not a bruising like you often heard of, but a proper fracture. "Worth busting your ass for" became shorthand in their home.

James stayed upright, vigilant against missing his role in this small theatre. When it was time for the rings he stepped forward. The task had been given to him because the twins were too old for it to be cute and young enough to not be trusted. Not that anyone blamed them, they were lively kids until all attention was on them, at which point they'd shut down, spill food, cry, any manner of thing. And James wanted this small job, cherished this inclusion. Somehow he'd always struggled to believe Martha really loved him, a carry-over from his own relationship with his dad, perhaps, where things were always left unspoken and affection was for women and weaklings. He loved Martha fearfully, fully – embers powerful with heat that never went out, but never flared into flame. And now today, when she looked over to him as though he was a bus arriving right on time, he felt that whatever she felt for him, it was good enough, it was good. He stepped forward on his good leg so he wouldn't falter.

Martha Junior married a man called Gez who'd broken his wrist rollerblading, his ankle skiing, his elbow jumping off at the apex of a playground swing and his foot bounding over a rock walking in the Black Mountains in Wales. There'd been a couple of other accidents along the way which he couldn't always remember, but every so often they'd come across something that would remind him and a new story would emerge. "But I thought you broke your foot in Wales," she'd say. And he'd reply, "Oh well I must have done it more than once. I definitely broke the left one skipping rope at a boxing gym." It made her suspicious because she couldn't imagine forgetting a break in this way, even if it did seem to happen more often to him than to the average man. Once, in an effort to keep track of all the stories, she'd drawn a crude outline of a man and marked in red pen each place he'd said he'd snapped. She'd never broken a bone herself, but she'd been close.

She straightened her collar and walked smartly up to meet him in front of the registrar. Over her shoulder she took another quick look at the kids, then swept her eyes up to Gez's face. She wondered if she held his hands for long enough, would his ossifying cartilage weave them together, her fingers the warp, his the weft. She was prepared to try.

Finders Keepers

"We all need to be more vigilant, don't we? Couldn't we, Anna? Be more vigilant?"

Mary asked nothing but rhetorical questions the day of the burglary. Diane seethed.

"I have my key." Anna held it between her finger and thumb, a witness, a crucifix purging the scene, heating up in her hands and threatening to bend: "I always use it." The back door had been jimmied, the TV-DVD taken, a laptop, some costume jewellery left lying around, that was it. Who cared.

"You have insurance, don't you?"

"Yes but that's not the point, is it? We've been invaded, haven't we? Someone broke in..."

"Yes they *broke* in..."

"You didn't double-lock. We told you. We told you to always double-lock the back door," Diane wouldn't even look at her, was stroking the seams of the frame that had been burst with a crowbar or a foot and a shoulder. She touched the warped door handle, hit by a brick the police thought, as if it was a dying someone's cheek.

"Look, I just don't see what the problem is. This sort of thing happens sometimes, it's no one's fault, it was a decision made by someone who isn't here and whom they're never going to catch so there's no point speculating." Anna trailed off, ready to move on.

Whoever it was hadn't made it upstairs, had been spooked by something, a neighbour maybe, a noise, so Anna's stuff hadn't been touched. The door of her room had stayed shut, her hand-washed white underwear still hanging along the top of the radiator.

Mary looked her dead in the eye, then at her ankle, then at the line of flat belly between her T-shirt and yoga pants. "We think it might be time for you to find somewhere else to stay." Anna immediately and resolutely decided that no, that was not going to happen.

This summer seemed to accumulate shit, becoming more and more leaden as it shambled along. After the accident the others in the company, the director, even Emma the programmer had said, "Take some time," "Think how nice it'll be to rest, to read, to recoup." The sorts of things said by people who pretended it was a choice. It was during previews for a dance production she was in, some strange piece based on the story of Rumpelstiltskin that was set in a housing compound in an unnamed Arabic country, and she'd rolled her ankle first one way, then another. It was her own stupid fault for trying to carry on, but someone had spread a rumour that there would be an agent in the crowd that night and she felt she owed it to herself, which was stupid because a mistake like that was amateur. Anna had told the rest of the company that she'd tried to carry on for their sake. She'd landed awkwardly, gotten up to finish the section then fallen the other way when she'd tried to put weight on the wrong side. If her ankle was a clock face, she'd pulled the ligaments forward six hours, then back six hours all in a matter of seconds. And it turned out the agent didn't show until opening night anyway.

She'd spent May applying for jobs, June getting none of them, and finally in July she'd started working in an independent petrol station because a friend had called in sick and she'd offered to cover her. They'd given her a couple of shifts that day, which turned into a few weeks of work, then they promised to keep her employed till August 31. It had seemed random and silly and just one of those things, but at some point, maybe when July dragged on as a wall of unending heat and frustration and petrol fumes, and Anna realised this was no joke but just a waste of fucking weeks and months, she'd tipped from shrugging it off to a growing fury at what had happened to her. Staying up nights made it easier, somehow. It ran her blood thin with anger and made her mornings grim, but the hours of electric light and the hot dead air outside encouraged the idea that she was making the most of it, of a bad situation. Truthfully she was making fuck all. "It" wasn't some sort of fertile field, some prolific substance, "it" was gas rainbows and lunch that came out of a wrapper and two room-mates that she could only call roommates at night, when she was finally alone, when she could mouth words in the dark and pretend she was screaming.

Now she could feel herself sagging and weakening while everything else lurched forward like poor clutch control. Six weeks on crutches, rest, then low-impact exercise – the end of everything, pretty much. If she lost this summer season, which she had, there was no coming back, any more than you could have twins and then just slide back into your leotard the next month. It was done. This knowledge, and the refusal of those around her to voice it, to agree with her about it, made her brittle, flinty. Her nails chipped easily, breaking off into splinters of kindling, and even in the sticky humidity she felt a static build-up fizzing at her edges as she gingerly walked across the forecourt at the end of each shift, holding her breath and imagining her sparks exploding everything around her, a fireball with her at the centre. It was company policy to always have two people on during an evening shift and for some reason her rota had been matched with a woman named Kelly, who made her say things like "don't know don't care" and "whatever" because engaging with her was too much of a risk. Kelly had small, darting eyes, fiercely braided hair and a volatility that made her almost always arrive late and leave early, usually with a fistful of candy bars plucked straight from the shelves. Kelly seemed perpetually ready for a fight and Anna couldn't tell if she hated her or was scared of her or both. Anna had told her about the burglary because it was dramatic enough to distract her from teasing drivers.

"How did they get in?" she asked.

"Broke the back door in. It was flimsy, plus Mary and Diane, my... the people I'm rooming with were too cheap to get a decent replacement. I bet it happens again. Now they know they missed the first floor."

"Where do you live again?"

"One of those streets alongside the park, the side near the water."

"Fuckin la-di-da."

"It's a nice house for sure."

Kelly glared, her little, dark eyes flicking back and forth. "Oh yeah?" She said it like a dare.

"Yeah well," as non-committal as Anna could muster.

"Sorry sir we don't accept forgeries," Kelly was suddenly saying to a man trying to pay for petrol and a frozen pizza through the service window. She slapped the note against the glass, "I can see where you've smudged the ink. I'll need to report you."

The man on the other end of Kelly's irritable boredom spluttered something about it not being his note, nothing to do with him, and Kelly slammed her fist and stood up, ready to really go.

After the police had left, after Mary and Diane had gone to bed without saying goodnight, Anna sat in the living room staring at the space left by the absent TV. Rotating her wrists produced pops like a clicking tongue that disapproved of her picking the flaky scales from her cracked heels. She'd made a little pile of tinder from the peelings and placed them on the thick spine of a book that was splayed upside down on the glass coffee table. Whichever one was reading it, whoever it was that had a friend who'd told them that they absolutely must read the hardcover version because it *read differently, in the hands*, would snatch it up one evening and be doused. She was planting herself, integrating herself into the space. She hadn't cleaned the bath in her en suite since she'd moved in, left its sides coated with whatever came off her, and evenings when they were out at some gallery thing or reading she went into their room and put on their clothes, bending and twisting in a mockery of their movements, rubbing herself into the fibres. In the kitchen she dug her long, bony fingers into the jars of rice and lentils, rinsed gulps of milk around in her mouth before depositing it back into the carton. She didn't know how this was going to end, if they would leave or finally force her out or some goddamn thing, but no matter what the space would still breathe her, and they'd have to scrub her away, and even still she'd linger in spaces they hadn't thought to look yet. She'd given up her own place long before the summer and she'd left the dance company to close around her absence, flattening her like a stone disappearing under water, arriving at Mary and Diane's with a backpack and a dread of autumn. The gas station paid enough for exactly nothing, and she knew with this leg she'd have no luck landing anything else. All she had was the house.

With the insurance money from the burglary they got an even bigger TV and an even newer laptop. Anna pretended not to notice Diane's face tightening when she asked to see it, opening the box and pulling it out. The two of them started going to bed earlier and earlier, shutting the bedroom door and then having longer and more agitated conversations behind it. Anna listened to them decide whose fault it was. At first it seemed like Mary's, because Anna and Mary knew each other from college. But then it tipped to Diane's side, because Diane had been the one to brush away Anna's insincere offer to pitch in for rent, to assure her that there was no need to schedule things, that Anna needed time to recover and was more than welcome to stay. Now Diane was paying for it with every day that Anna came home with another gas-smelling $47.50 in her pocket that she added to the money belt she'd started wearing everywhere she went, even the toilet.

"How's the apartment hunting going?" Diane asked her miserably.

Mary watched from across the room and Anna could feel the coaching and whispered threats that propped up the question. Poor Diane. It was half seven. If they went into the bedroom by 8 p.m., it wouldn't be the first time. Anna opened the box of pizza she'd brought home with her and picked up the second to last lukewarm piece. The biodegradable box oozed grease on to the countertop and Anna ate without a plate, lowering the slice into her mouth and feeling the distant, tiny thud of diced tomato and green pepper falling on the kitchen floor next to her bare feet.

"Well, it's not really a renter's market is it," she said, chewing with her mouth open.

"It's just about the end of the month and—"

"There's eleven days till the end of the month."

"Exactly. And now is when places are opening up for next month. Mary and I think—"

"Mary, did you borrow my black shirt? With the bit around the collar?" She had no black shirt with a bit around the collar, and they all knew it.

Mary walked behind the sofa and placed her hands carefully on the back, "No Anna, I haven't borrowed your shirt. What can we do to help make this easier?" she asked quietly.

"I don't mind if you took it, but just ask first, yeah? It's no big deal, I just like to know."

Anna sucked her fingertips and then folded up the last slice into thirds, like a letter going into an envelope. Mary and Diane with their master's degrees in Business Management. Mary and Diane who'd managed to stay together even during the post-college, mortifying pixie haircut and unemployed years. Mary and Diane with their mortgage and their motto: we made it. Emphasis on the "we". Emphasis on the "made". Emphasis on the "it".

Mary and Diane had left at 5 p.m. to go do whatever it was they did when they went away for the weekend: pre-theatre, a play, The Prince Regent. Or a Harvester, a Hollywood blockbuster and hash smoked out of a little wooden pipe she'd found one morning on the breakfast bar along with red-wine rings and the scrunched-up foil and wrapper from a triple-pack of Rolos. It was three weeks after the burglary, and the letter they'd slid under her door used words like "untenable", "difficult" and "disappointed". She'd forced their hands, apparently. As if she'd hovered over them, guided their fingers over the keyboard, tap-tap-tapping their instructions for her eviction.

The note outlined a three-step plan. She had to one, take the roll of bin bags they'd left for her in the hallway; two, fill them up with her stuff; and three, leave by the end of the weekend. They would give her some space while she cleared out. But the bin bags were cheap, tore at the mere hint of a hard edge, dribbling her sock-stuffed shoes down the stairs. She raged at this, tore at the bags till her hands smelt of chemical-smoked plastic. She threw her things from the fifth step down to the front door, knocking a spider plant out of its pot and spilling soil into the gaps in the hardwood floors. This set her off even more, her heels striking the ground like hammers, the walls and cupboard doors flimsy under her hands like cheap cardboard. Too angry to stay in one place, she was unable to even direct her anger. She decided to start again in the morning and took a long shower to try and extinguish the hot flames of fury licking up her spine, up into the back of her throat. None of this was even remotely fair.

When the morning came a sullenness layered overtop of everything else, and she refused to clean, to pack; she opened the doors to let the late summer breeze blow the dirt deeper into the floorboards, wafting pollen and grass into the hall. She sat on the porch drinking the last of Diane's Bombay Sapphire with Diet Sprite, gripping the pint glass hard till the gin got warm and the fizz from the mixer was flattened. She made three bags of popcorn, ate one and threw the rest on to the lawn. Birds gathered quickly, cawing and clapping. They hung on expectantly, even began roosting in the horse chestnut, splattering branches and the ground underneath chalky white and sputum green.

She drank the wine they used for cooking, and when that was gone she went down into the basement to start in on their special bottles, the ones they were probably saving for anniversaries and birthdays and promotions. She had one more entire day, so she got to work fast. If they were going to force her out, she would leave as much of herself here as possible.

In Diane and Mary's room she noticed that they'd cleared out a lot more stuff than could be expected for going away for the weekend. Special things, expensive things, had been taken, put somewhere away from her. Jewellery, cashmere, leather shoes. The closets were half-full, the vanity unusually bare. This inflamed her. She tried to be methodical, but there was no method. She was all fingers and flying spit – a stack of towels thrown into the bath and then the taps turned on, a direct hit from a glass candleholder in the centre of a propped-up mirror. She didn't waste time mussing sheets or pissing on the carpet – she mashed lipsticks into walls, poured perfume into the underwear drawer, beat a frozen fish into the ceramic stovetop until scaly shards flew everywhere, melting slowly in trails that slid between cabinets.

She got tired after lunch. It was hard to sustain the fury. So she lay on the ground and mantra'd herself into a shallow sleep. This wasn't *theirs*, it wasn't their house, these weren't their things. Because they'd done nothing to deserve it. Ownership was earned.

She woke up again suddenly, a smell of fish in the air, someone knocking at the door. It was just after 4 p.m. Lifting her head off the living room carpet made it feel like it was coming apart, and the dripping in the kitchen, which had grown more insistent, beat out the pounding of her heart in her temples.

"I just wanted to check you were alright."

"Who are you?"

The middle-aged woman peered at Anna through the inch-gap left by the front door's security chain. She had the wide black eyes and turned-up nose of a nocturnal mammal. She skittered on the porch, umming and ahing.

"I'm across from you," she pointed her finger beyond Anna's shoulder, which she followed down the hall towards the wide-open back door that Anna couldn't remember opening, "and I heard about the burglary so wanted to check everything was, um, okay."

Anna smiled, then gently shut the door in her neighbour's face. She went to the back door for relief from the stifling heat, leant on it, let the breeze carry her belches away. Outside clouds covered the sky from the ground up, presumably closing in for a storm. Her eyesight glitched, hands and knees trembled, sweat came till she puked, scorched-tasting. One by one each anomaly left her and she felt much better, until the sounds of drawers being opened and closed upstairs set her heart racing again, anger refluxing.

She sidled up the stairs with her back to the wall, scoping as much of the first floor as she possibly could with one eye closed for focus, the walls still tilting woozily. Noises from Mary and Diane's en suite, like a toothbrush cup falling into the sink or the bath. Anna knew what she'd say. She'd say, "Fuck you," "Get out," "I mean it," and "It's mine." But when she opened the door and saw Kelly from the petrol station bent over a laundry basket, skimming through a pile of silk dry-cleaning, mainly strappy vests, the words felt wrong till they felt right.

"What the fuck?"

Kelly froze, then rounded.

"What?" she said, completely brazen.

"What do you mean, *what*? Get the fuck out of here!"

"No."

"What? Who do you think you are? Why are you even here?"

"You said they had stuff, had got new stuff. The door wasn't locked."

"Yes it was."

"Not locked enough," she laughed, actually laughed. Then in a whiny, pissy little voice, "Didn't double-lock, did you?"

"Kelly get the fuck out of here."

She rushed at Anna, twisting her T-shirt into a tight ring, her nails pinching and pulling at her chest.

"Do you think it matters that you're here?" she breathed into Anna's neck. "Do you think I didn't think about stepping on your face when I walked straight past you? Shut the fuck up."

Kelly shoved her away, both hands into her diaphragm, and Anna was winded by the force and the clashing smells of CK One and body butter and gas and Red Bull.

She heaved out, "I'm not leaving, I'm not going to leave and let you take your pick."

"Do what you want," Kelly started to open and reopen the bathroom drawers and cupboards, convinced that she might see something that wasn't there two seconds ago.

"You won't find anything. They took it all with them." Not that she wanted weed or Valium anyway. It was too slow, too oozy. It took the purpose out of her anger.

Anna crawled out of the bathroom, used Mary and Diane's bed to winch herself up, then went to her room. Kelly obviously hadn't been in here yet because her wardrobe doors were open, revealing pristinely hung shirts, jackets, jeans and scarves. When she bent down to get the three-litre bottle of Russian Standard from under her bed, she felt muscle move against rib in a spasm that made her jerk upright again. She tightened the money belt that was, thankfully, still around her waist and walked towards the sounds of Kelly's pointless ransacking.

"What is this shit?" She hurled a bottle of talcum at the floor. It bounced and poofed like a smoke pellet. "Not even my fucking nanna. This place is a shithole. It fucking reeks."

"What do you expect from a pair of prissy cunts," Anna went into the bathroom, picked up the plastic toothbrush cup and a smudged glass and filled them up till they spilt. "You want a drink?"

"Whatever," Kelly grabbed the glass, took a mouthful, balked, then took another. Anna went to the bed, lay down on the duvet and rested the cup on her chest.

"They took everything with them. There's nothing here," she said again.

The money belt was digging into her, but the thick duvet and soft mattress masked the bump at the small of her back.

"Shut your hole," Kelly started rummaging again.

Anna snorted. "Whatever will be, will be" in her head. Fucking Doris Day.

Kelly worked methodically around the room, opening everything. Then in one drawer, "passports".

Anna sat up on one elbow, holding the vodka on the sharpest part of her hip bone.

"Let's see the photos, pass them here."

Kelly opened one of the blue books at the photo page and took it as close to Anna's nose as she could, forcing her to sit up some more.

"Ha! She looks ridiculous!" Diane's hair was long at the sides, short on top, almost military. Her light eyes blending into her pale skin and the white background.

Anna took a celebratory, minty sip. Fuck Diane. Kelly took the passport back and put it in her back pocket, then rested on the back of a chair.

"You're a dancer, right?"

"Yeah, well..."

"Do something," Kelly said. "Do a dance or something."

"I'm not doing shit for you."

"*Look at me I'm a flat-chested twat, such a pretty little flower,*"

Kelly made an imaginary arbour with her arms above her head, got as high on her toes as she could.

Anna watched her calf muscles get round, her thighs tensing along with the rest of her body, opening out and lengthening for a moment before sagging back into formless nothing when she dropped on to her flat feet and sat back down on the chair.

Kelly needed distraction, needed to be drawn away like a toddler. When she wasn't looking Anna tipped the plastic cup over her shoulder, let it run into the bedcover. Anna got up and took the second passport and showed Kelly the photo page. Putting her thumb over the date she asked, "Guess how old this one is?"

Kelly guessed eleven years too old. Haw-haw. It was clear to Anna now, the party was over. The house reeked of fish and booze and damp and anger. The spinning and whirring that had been mostly pent up in her mind was bleeding out into her body, and the more her muscles and head ached, the more her mind sharpened. It was the end of August, it was the evening, it was that brief, splitting time when something was about to crack off, the silence just before the phone rings. But Kelly was just getting going; it was Friday night for Kelly. She was flipping through Mary's passport and Anna hefted the bottle of vodka over and topped up both their cups. Before Kelly accepted one she idly tore two pages down the middle, not detaching them completely.

"You could have sold that," Anna said, tipping out the contents of her own cup next to the nightstand, where it seeped into the off-white carpet immediately.

"Could not."

"You probably could've. Sell the other one."

"I'm going to fucking use it."

Anna snorted. "Sure. Mexico in disguise. What are you, a spy? *Why*, you idiot? What's wrong with your own fucking passport?"

"Haven't got one."

"Sell it or leave it alone."

Kelly wriggled upwards from the chair and went to the bed. Anna leant back on the wall, letting her move away. The money belt was constricting. It felt tight and growing tighter and she was heating up, slowly getting red. She could maybe manage one more cup. Kelly was only two-thirds of the way through hers, but Anna topped them both up anyway. She flopped on the bed next to Kelly, hoping to encourage her to stay put. There was a lamp on the nightstand that had withstood most of the carnage, only losing its navy blue shade. The bulb stuck up like a periscope. Anna reached down and unplugged it from the wall.

When Kelly's cup was still half-full she started to get restless, bored. She stood up and started going through the same drawers she'd gone through twenty minutes earlier, sloppier this time but also more angry. As Kelly bent down to reach the bottom dresser drawer, the one where she knew there was fuck all apart from a load of holey jumpers and a couple of pairs of stretched-out black leggings, Anna took one lukewarm quick sip, the way you might dig your fingernails into your palm while a nurse takes blood from the other arm, and then swung the lamp across the back of Kelly's head. She'd never done something like that before and although she thought the chances were excellent that Kelly would simply fall over and then get up and go fucking ballistic, it actually seemed to work. She felt it up her arm like a clean racquet ball hit, strong with a follow-through. Kelly slammed forward, hit her chest off the dresser, and then ended up on the floor, still breathing, a bit of blood – not much – but certainly out. Anna's hand went straight to the money belt, practically down her trousers. Holding on to herself, she walked out of the room and into her own room, where she took only the bare essentials, light enough to not rip the piece-of-shit bags, and threw the cup of vodka over the remaining clothes hanging in the closet. She walked down the stairs and out the back door, leaving it wide open.

She picked up a pebble from the back lawn and threw it in the direction of the nosy neighbour, setting the security light off and the curtains twitching. She'd walk into town, down the middle of empty roads. She'd find the seams and cleave the night apart.

The Lesser of Two Evils

The river wasn't that far from the main road, but the heavy rain made the water roar as it flowed over trees that had succumbed on both banks, shushing the sound of any cars that might be passing this early on a Monday morning. He was standing in the middle of the bridge that crossed into the park, looking over the edge of the railing, and so Theresa turned her head to try and glimpse whatever it was he'd spotted. Perhaps it was a heron; they were often to be seen where the river shallowed at the bend before it flowed on past the old sewage treatment plant, out towards a grey basin where it thickened and could settle into itself, becoming fat and slow and single-minded. But the water was rough today and the herons would know it'd be tough to spot a fish under all the froth and foam churned from flooded burns and marsh plains. Theresa didn't stop but definitely slowed her pace when the man swung one of his Marks & Spencer plastic bags (she could tell from the black-and-white stripe design) from down by his side, all the way up and over his head, launching it into the water below, where it sank almost immediately under the speeding current. He walked away then, not looking back, over the bridge and into the park. She checked her watch: 6:44. She looked skyward for a second and tested her memory to recall his details: black shoes. Trainers? Not sure. Black trousers. Jeans? Not sure. Black top. A coat with a collar. Black hair, cut short at the neck. She hadn't seen his face and she'd guess 5'8" although he could have been taller, it was hard to tell. He'd walked away with one bag. What did he need to keep and what was he throwing away? Or was he walking further down the river to separate his disposal of whatever was in those two bags? And Marks & Spencer wasn't even open yet.

In the office she told Marion because Joanne wasn't in yet. She blinked her eyes before Theresa had even finished talking, for full effect. "So?" She was notoriously useless for this kind of thing.

"Weird, right? What's in the bag?"

"How will you ever find the answer to that question, Theresa?"

"…I won't. I'm just wondering about it, it was a strange thing to see."

Whatever spark came to life when they talked about budgets and catering plans receded further behind the blue slate wall of Marion's gaze. She shrugged theatrically.

"Enough's going on that we *can* answer, I think. Right? Can you check these catering plans and tell me which one you think we should go for?"

Without taking her eyes from Theresa's face Marion pulled over two packages of paper, each held together in the top right corner with a paper clip, which was better than clipping the left corner, because people read from left to right and top to bottom, so affixing the paper at the top right allowed for uninterrupted reading. Theresa looked more closely. The files were labelled "State Justice Visit Catering Plan Option A" and "State Justice Visit Catering Plan B".

Theresa was fond of talking through her thinking so she said, "Well it's an important visit and A comes with those nice little cakes… do you remember we had them at the AGM reception? But B would keep us under budget. We should probably confirm with Joanne. I would say A but let's double-check with Joanne. Joanne can be the decider in case we're split, you and I. Yes, let's do that."

An old boyfriend of hers had found these monologues particularly irritating: *Just do the working in your head! You're like a toddler doing math on their fingers*, which she resented because he'd been so anally retentive, and wouldn't share anything of what he was thinking until it was too late and it all came oozing out of him like infected earwax. She could tell that Marion was maybe thinking something similar but she didn't care. She liked to talk things through, she was a list maker, a recipe follower, a cinema talker – her oohs and aahs, jumps and laughs only made the film more real for other people who felt they had to keep their reactions in. She was more natural in her responses, and always open. More people should be that way, she thought.

Joanne said Menu A as well, but only after Theresa had made the point about the cakes, which put her in a good mood for the rest of the day. Joanne was also much more interested in the man with the bags, as Theresa had known she would be, and even started to keep a tab of local news open on her desktop so she could periodically check for any stories that might feasibly have a connection. Joanne was always quick to get in on a game, to *take part*, whatever that looked like. Sometimes her intensity had an edge, but Theresa felt the situation certainly warranted some suspicion. It seemed like a great length to go to for commonplace littering.

"It's suspicious, no doubt about it," Joanne agreed.

Theresa nodded triumphantly while Marion pretended not to listen. But by the end of the day nothing had been posted; there was a story about an elderly man who was knocked down outside the library by a bicycle food-delivery service worker, but he was expected to make a full recovery and the food-delivery service had quickly expressed appropriate sympathy. Nothing about the river and the mysterious hurling. She walked home the same way, saw absolutely nothing out of order, made instant rice with a slick packet of peanut sauce that took seven tries to tear, and ate it in front of Zeffirelli's *Romeo and Juliet*. "Much too young; he must have needed special permission to film her naked, she's a *child*," she said to no one.

The next morning she woke with swollen glands. They practically radiated out of her neck. Her throat was like sandpaper and she felt a powerful throbbing, as if her head was wrapped in elastic bands. She got as far as halfway through her shower before crawling back to bed. Joanne was no good for this, so she sent a businesslike text to Marion and then turned her phone off and boiled a kettle. She filled it up well past the greyish line that marked her usual fill: "This is no time to monkey around; with a sore throat, if you don't nip it in the bud, you're doomed," she croaked into the cabinet. After twenty hours of sleep and a packet and a half of throat lozenges she appeared at work again, wan and tremulous and maybe luminous rather than damp, she hoped.

"I've been waiting for you! Where have you been?" Joanne hissed.

"I wasn't feeling so well, I sent Marion a message..."

"Theresa, it was a *child*."

Without understanding why, Theresa put her hand out, palm up, between Joanne and herself. "I don't want to know what you mean," she started saying, but it was too late.

"There was a *child* in the bag," Joanne said again.

"I have no idea what you – on the bridge? No. That man? No." Then, "Where's Marion?" And then again, "*No*."

"She's just across the road getting coffee because the machine is out of milk powder again, for the hundredth time this week. Okay, I shouldn't have said a child. I'm sorry. But close. There was a puppy in the bag that he threw. Which is really a child dog."

Theresa had a ringing in her ears. It could have been from her sinuses, swollen and beating in time with her heart. Or it could have been from the image that swam into view of pink and tender skin, soft knees and elbows stretching plastic thin enough to see through.

"I think I'm going to be sick."

"Let's not tell Marion. It might upset her."

She'd gone home again afterwards. Joanne had insisted and Theresa couldn't even look at her to protest. She went to bed at 2 p.m. after eating a can of tomatoes, the only thing that had appealed to her in any way, and slept like a stone until she woke with a start at 7 a.m. the next day. She felt as if her glands had swollen so much they were meeting in the middle, clogging the back of her throat and bringing water to her eyes. It was hard to swallow, and her ears felt like they needed to pop, but she felt she'd turned a corner, and couldn't bear being in the flat for another day. She couldn't bring herself to pass the river. She went the quick way to work, along the main road, and got splashed by a black cab turning a corner. She took her tights off when she got to the office and hung them on the radiator, the feet hanging stiffly from the muddy water, as the nylon slowly dried to a crisp. When Marion got in Theresa expected her to say something, but all she did was double-take Theresa's pale legs.

Theresa opened up a weather forecast site and every time her nausea crept up she forced herself to stare at the little rain icon. This was something she did every so often; something about the shade of grey-blue the site used for the raindrops, and the way the animated cloud seemed to drift across the screen without ever actually moving, helped. It was a fail-safe soothing technique whose power she didn't dare dilute by using it too often. At eleven o'clock they had their check-in scheduled, and as usual no one wanted to be the first to get up and as usual at five past eleven Marion announced she was just getting a coffee first and then just as she came back with it Joanne needed to run to the ladies' and at eight past they finally all turned from their desks as a unit and moved to huddle on three overstuffed pieces of office furniture that could be used as seating, footrests or side tables, at a cost of £950 each. They were metres away from their desks.

"So the state visit is only four weeks away, which means it's crunch time."

"Crunch time?"

"A matter of urgency," Marion hissed crisply in Joanne's direction. Theresa began filling in a medium-sized rectangle with her blue biro between two lines on her pad of paper. A muted "ping" made Joanne leap back to her desk. Marion pursed her lips.

"Sorry. But there's a sale on duvet covers until Sunday, if anyone is interested. Oh my god!"

"I've loads of duvet covers, but thanks," murmured Theresa, one-third of the way through her rectangle.

"No! I've just checked the news, oh my god."

Even Marion wanted in, spinning round to see Joanne reading off her screen.

"Close your ears if you don't want to know."

"For god's sake just tell us," Marion's patience could only be stretched so far.

"It was babies. *Plural.*"

"Babies?"

"Kittens. I thought it was puppies? But the man, he worked at a vet's and it was kittens and he's been fired but also charged. Three baby kittens. So yes, babies."

"Joanne what are you saying? It was a dog? A dog that had died?"

"I didn't say that!" And then in response to Theresa's look, "No I didn't!" Joanne insisted, "What are you talking about? I didn't."

"What is *wrong* with you, Joanne?" This came forcefully from Marion but expressed Theresa's feelings perfectly.

"I'm distraught. Baby kittens. It says here he's only worked there three months. What if he only got the job so he could be close – oh, it's too horrible," she moaned, actually wringing her hands.

"You do understand the difference though don't you? Between a baby and a kitten?"

"What? What difference?"

Theresa watched Marion's face as she struggled to find

words appropriate for the professional setting, mentally recalling the hundreds of sober PowerPoint slides from Equality and Diversity training that had flashed on and on in an endless stream, with the taste of crumbling macaroons and stale coffee in the back of her throat.

"People are just *awful*, aren't they? And you can never tell. I read about a surgeon who would cauterise his initials into his patients. And there's the phantom person in this building that left a" – she mouthed the next word – "*poo* in one of the bathroom sinks."

"When did that happen?" Marion was temporarily distracted by this.

"It was before my time but can you even imagine? It was a health and safety issue, they had to send everyone home for the day. They never did find out who it was."

This fact hung in the air, pointless and so impossible to respond to.

"Anyway, they've got CCTV footage of him. The man that threw away the babies. They've blurred his face and the bag, see?" She gestured for the pair of them to gather round her computer but neither of them moved. "I'm sure you can see the shape of them."

"Joanne, stop it." Theresa tried to make her voice steady and sure to let her know how serious she was about shutting this topic down.

"I just feel desperate about it. Tiny. They must have been tiny. Innocent. What's wrong with him?"

"Shall we move on Joanne?"

For the rest of the day every time Joanne said anything about anything Marion made a face. And in the kitchen at lunchtime she caught Theresa's eye and just shook her head. Joanne hadn't raised the subject again but it was clear that she'd had a conversation with someone about it later in the afternoon, a more amiable audience maybe, because she strode back into the office with her "My kingdom for a cuppa" mug hanging empty off a finger, coffee forgotten, and a mass email appeared ten minutes later announcing the theme for this year's Christmas appeal: Cats Protection League.

Theresa's dreams squirmed. Earth writhed; flesh bubbled with unseen life. By the weekend, with the rain still incessant, roads and houses had begun to flood. On Monday she considered calling in sick but forlornly thought of the days she'd been actually sick, and felt worse somehow trying to stretch out that experience. She walked past the river, tentatively, but when she got there and registered the figure in the deep-blue mac, she charged ahead, concern and sensitivity forgotten.

"Joanne, I know you don't live around here!" was what came out, too shrill, too desperate. Theresa looked down at her arm with curious detachment to see her left hand firmly pressing into Joanne's coat.

"Oh, but I do. Or, I was. I mean, I was here. I mean, last night. So I'm walking in this way too. Have you come to... see?"

"This is how I get to work, Joanne. What are you doing here?"

"Commuting!" she wrenched herself away from Theresa and walked closer to the edge of the bridge, peering over and down.

"This isn't right Joanne, it's not healthy."

"You don't... I never win anything, never been a part of anything, and you just walked to work one day and there you have it. But you won't even acknowledge what you saw!"

Joanne stood on her tiptoes. Theresa was convinced her glasses were going to fall off her face and into the water that had risen even further up the banks since she'd last seen it.

"Do you ever find yourself hoping to spot a body in a siding when you're sat in a window seat on the train?"

Theresa moved a little closer, reaching out for Joanne's coat again.

"I suppose I've wondered how I'd react in an emergency, is that the kind of thing that you mean?"

"No I mean, that *you're* the one that spots it. You get to be the one."

"Joanne, what were you doing last night?" It occurred to Theresa that perhaps she was drunk, oddly focused on whatever story was going on in her head that she wasn't sharing properly.

"It was a date. I was on a date. A blind date."

"That sounds fun," she knew she sounded patronising but Theresa just wanted to pull Joanne away from the water, "where did you go?"

"We met in the park and just went for a walk."

"What, last night?"

"Yeah, we just walked around for an hour or so and then we went back to his."

"You went back to his? After a walk in the rain?" It was coming out all wrong and she sounded peevish, but Joanne didn't seem bothered.

"You've got to speculate to accumulate, Theresa," she said, finally turning away from the railing.

At work Joanne was quiet, put her headphones in and seemed to spend the day endlessly typing. Theresa wondered about what she'd said, about winning things, about witnessing things.

They met at the mirrors in the ladies' loos later after lunch. Joanne had her phone, which seemed unhygienic to Theresa. "He's been texting me all morning."

"Who?"

"The guy I was with last night."

"Made an impression, did you?"

"I can't tell. Yes, probably. He's saying that I left my scarf and do I want to come and pick it up."

"Sounds like an excuse to me. At college there was a guy who had this serious crush on me and once he messaged me to ask if I wanted to come round to get a can of juice I'd left at a party he'd had. He was such a wimp. Not cute at all," she caught herself then said, "but it was very sweet. I just didn't fancy him."

"Oh I fancy him, he's very, um, charismatic. He's got really small eyes but they're expressive, do you know what I mean?"

Theresa really didn't so she made a list: Wednesday 6:44 a.m., black shoes, black trousers, dark top, dark coat with a collar, dark hair cut short at the neck, 5'8". She put it in an email and sent it to Joanne, across the eight inches or so that separated the edges of their computer monitors. When she heard Joanne's intake of breath after a few clicks, Theresa stood up and announced she had an errand to run and might not be back for the rest of the day. She left without looking back, taking the stairs instead of the elevator to send the blood pumping in her ears down into her legs.

Who Knows What's Out There

It was the Friday before a long weekend and to Alex everything felt like it was shutting down. Death couldn't correspond to a calendar, right? Did priests go on caravan holidays to the coast like everyone else? Not that Alex had religion, but the notion of a funeral without a religious figure seemed confusing to her, so she'd looked online for someone who seemed competent. Luckily the man now weaving through the draughty hall, holding each person's hand with both of his for a beat or two, fit the bill. Her own involvement in the few funerals she'd experienced was still tinged with self-centredness, like the time she got her period at her former boss's wake, black folds of a dress invisibly wet. Or the time her college boyfriend's somewhat famous author father had been killed in a drunk-driver hit-and-run and her constant awareness of the larger crowd and her position in the front line had her shifting her profile further and further to the left till she'd completed a near semicircle around the open grave as family members queued to sprinkle dirt.

Alex decided that she should be the one to start the round of applause. When they thanked the caterer and the people that did the readings it would be her job to start it. She'd seen it before, how the sound could break the tension. It would make them all feel better or at least create some noise to counter the hush. Except that later she remembered the idea had come from Princess Diana's funeral and that was probably why it had sounded so deviant and uncertain in the rec room of the church. She'd uncrossed her ankles, thinking to add a standing ovation, but had thankfully caught herself at the last moment.

Later, as they all mingled around the unfolded metal legs of plastic tables covered with translucent vinyl tablecloths, Alex stacked four cheese puffs on a paper plate before registering the dessert table. Someone plucked the tip of her elbow, as though trying to pinch it off; she turned to look down at her Aunt Kath, now short one sister but not seeming too broken up about it, wrinkled and tenderised with age, loose skin trembling and giving off tiny spores of powder. Alex's sister Maria stood next to her, licking her lips to clear all signs of the mini quiche she'd been nibbling, dislodging a buttery crumb which drifted down to her black three-quarter-length sleeve like a particularly large chunk of dandruff.

"Who did you come with?" Aunt Kath demanded.

"Maria drove."

"I see. Did you have to travel far?"

"Well, yes, we came from the city," Maria said.

"You did?"

"That's where we stay, Katherine. For a few years now."

Alex thought it felt strange not calling her Aunty Kath, made her feel wider somehow, like she was taking up more space than she would have otherwise.

It was left to Alex and Maria to clear the buffet debris into large black bin bags. Everyone else had gone to the pub or home or to another funeral. Some of them just seemed to travel around bidding fare-thee-well to folk for three or four days of a week. An unfortunate friend group maybe, or just sociable enough to know lots of people who were all heading in the same direction. Alex figured she'd never cast her net that wide. Maria was headed down the wrong road: she sent her cleaner Christmas cards and still kept up with exes. "No kids no worries" was Alex's motto, but Maria, with her two girls, skinny-legged dynamos, said that wasn't true either. "You're not alone in this world, and don't wish you were," she'd say. Alex wanted to be alone, hated the noise of neighbours on a Sunday morning, crossed streets to avoid strangers. She ran a tight ship, as she described it to herself. Secrets sustained her, and for no good reason either. She'd been a smoker for two years in adolescence without a soul knowing, was taking bass lessons she'd told no one about and regularly flew cross-country for work, maintaining the mundane texting that seemed to soothe Maria. *Got a stupid headache. Might just stay in for a bath and read my book. Say hi to the girls and I'll see you next week.*

"Kath was a bad bitch in her day," Alex said, tossing a stack of paper plates damp with grease into the third and final bin bag. They couldn't even be recycled, would decay at a glacial pace, outdoing anyone who had eaten off them today in terms of life experience.

"Who told you that?" Maria was immediately sceptical; this type of person didn't actually exist in real life, in her real life.

"Geraldine. She didn't stick about to help tidy either." Another stack of cups with leafy shades of lipstick round the rims cascaded into a bag.

"What exactly did she say?" asked Maria.

"Oh, just stuff about when Kath was young. This and that."

"But how did you get 'bad bitch' from 'this and that'?"

"Geraldine just used certain words, and you can tell can't you, when someone's trying to say something about a person without actually saying it out loud because they want to be subtle or in case they get in trouble. Like 'efficient'. If anyone ever uses the word 'efficient' to describe a person you know they really mean 'cunt'."

"That's rubbish. I used to call people at work efficient all the time. And I never meant *that*. Well, nothing that harsh anyway. In your world what word is a stand-in for bad bitch?"

"Capable."

Maria, knowing nothing more about the conversation with Geraldine, had to nod her head in agreement. She couldn't understand things in any way other than the plain, simple truth, and she just didn't have what she needed here.

In 1972 Kath was insisting on Katherine because it sounded more professional. She'd been a nanny for four years already and was convinced her reputation warranted a nice family, in the nice houses on Park Street, with the nice children who wore blazers and caps to school and never walked around barefoot, not even in their own gardens. She spent most evenings before she fell asleep rewriting the day's events. Her bed was a thin single, a dismal mattress that poked into her in odd places, prompting these rewrites to last for hours. Version Two: Tommy had not brought home a salamander with three legs in his schoolbag because he knew she'd have to clean it out; Mr Chiltern, Mr Don't-Mind-if-I-Do, had broken his leg in three places tripping over a chair as a result of trying to brush against her breast, instead of just slipping slightly and laughing as if everything in his life was endlessly amusing; her period had arrived promptly instead of being now six days late. She put her hand on her abdomen, and then lightly between her legs. *Hurry up, hurry up.* She stared at the small desk with the thin drawer along its front across from her bed. Money, she thought. I want money.

Her mother used to say, "What's wrong with 'Kath'?"

"Nothing's wrong with it. But you named me Katherine for a reason didn't you?"

"After your Aunty Kath. It's a nice thing to share."

"She chose Kath; I choose Katherine."

She calculated that she'd worked for the Chiltern family for 1,216 days, after every one of which she'd gone to sleep to the smell of cheap offcuts fried in flour and too much butter.

The next day, May 17, 1972, Kath awoke atop a spongy crimson patch of sheet, ran through four separate prayers of thanks to four different saints, each with their own purview, quickly got dressed, and went downstairs to announce her imminent departure. She'd been ignoring the card in the post office window advertising for an au pair because it had sounded complicated and hot: *Nanny needed. Four months. Two toddlers. Outside Madrid. Send a letter of reference to: Rose Cottage, Lindersfield.* She didn't understand how the address could be so short and was pretty sure Madrid would be sticky for sixteen weeks even if it was near the sea and she wasn't sure it was. But when she walked past the house on a Sunday afternoon, purposefully taking a detour so she could assess their situation, and couldn't see the front door because of the high walls and long gravelled drive, she knew, at the very least, the job was what she deserved. She got a surprisingly good reference from Mrs Chiltern, which made her wonder if she was all too aware of her husband's wandering hands. A meeting with the two toddlers was set up quickly after that. They were leaving for Spain in less than two weeks and the hiring process had been very tiresome according to the young Mrs Brown who, despite bearing this frustration, had seemed energetic and friendly enough.

Rachel was seven and Sarah was five, too old for toddling as far as Kath was concerned, but Mrs B explained they advertised for the position every year and hadn't got round to changing the wording, or the card for that matter. She uncrossed and recrossed her legs and tapped her cigarette.

"Spend the afternoon together and see what you think."

So the kids would decide.

Rachel had long dark hair and wrinkly knees, as if she spent an inordinate amount of time in puddles. Unlike her sister, she looked every adult directly in the eyes. Mrs B went into the kitchen and stayed there, letting Kath and the kids size each other up.

"What games do you like to play, Sarah?"

"Oh, she likes to pretend she has friends."

Well, Rachel was clearly a bitch.

"Are you looking forward to the summer?"

"I suppose so. Are you coming with us?"

"That's up to your mother. I'd like to."

"How often do you wash your hands?"

"Whenever I need to."

"Because our last nanny didn't even wash her hands after she'd been to the bathroom. And you touch your fanny when you're in the bathroom. You should always wash your hands after you touch your fanny."

Kath felt the colour rise up her face even as she tried to hold it down.

"Do you know what they call a fanny in America?" she murmured, quiet enough for Mrs Brown not to hear, loud enough for Rachel, indistinct enough to get Sarah's sidelong look.

"What?" Rachel scoffed. She tried to hide it but she clearly didn't relish not knowing, and eyed Kath carefully.

"A mind-your-own-business."

"You've never even been to America," she said, her voice dripping scorn.

"Sarah, that's a really lovely drawing," Kath said over Rachel's shoulder, ignoring Rachel's comment, knowing then that she'd hooked her. Rachel flounced into the kitchen to announce she was hungry, and that she liked Katherine's pretty blue shoes.

They arrived in Madrid at night, sweating and fussy and exhausted. Katherine gaped at the public square full of families eating dinner close to midnight, their children still running around. Glasses of drink, full, glittering and ruby-coloured, caught her attention as she gazed down at the street from the second-floor apartment. She was meant to be off-duty by 9 p.m., but she'd been told a travel day was obviously different. A screech from the Mrs made her leap to the bags, the bathing, the quick mental map of what was needed to get the breakfast going in the morning. When she finally fell into bed she was bone-tired, and could still hear cutlery and chatter from outside. In the morning Sarah was in bed with her, curled around the pillow like a kitten, giving off the clean-linen smell of children's perspiration.

When Maria picked up the mail that afternoon, there was a fat letter with a faint stamp in place of a return address. She sliced it open with a ballpoint pen and read the first lines of the first page, sighed and made a mental note to call Alex once the girls were in bed. Then she neatly closed the cover of her mind's jotter and set her attention to dinner preparations. The children had been at their father's for the weekend and would be incapable of not talking in a stream of hyperactive sentences until at least tomorrow.

"So how was it?" he asked when he dropped them off.

"Coats and bags don't live in the hallway!" she bellowed. Then, "It was fine, I guess. I don't know, it was a funeral. It was weird."

It irritated her beyond anything else in her life that she could be this inarticulate, especially in front of him.

"They're emotional, it's emotional."

It was a relief to hear him sound just as dumb.

"We heard this weird story about when our Aunty Kath was young."

"I don't know if I ever met her. Does she live in the sticks?"

"She used to. She lives closer now. In a home."

The summer of '72 passed slowly, especially after July when the city emptied itself out and Mrs B found a summer school for the two children to work on their languages. Kath cleaned, ate, napped and walked the endless loop from apartment to school to apartment to school. At first Rachel had become very quiet after realising she could less easily manipulate her classmates because her Spanish was so poor. And she seemed to have developed a fancy for a boy she called David, whom she would shout after sometimes when Kath was collecting her at the school gates. Each time he would ignore her until one day he turned and said, pointedly, "Dav-*id*, Dav-*id*." Rachel had winced like she might cry but she'd sucked in her cheeks, choosing, Kath thought, to cry in private, which Kath respected immensely. But when she read the girls a story before bed, she couldn't resist inserting a character called David and felt Rachel writhe in fury and misery under the thin cover. Only nine days until they left this hot and confusing place that was too bright with blooming fuchsias, that made their clothes stiff-dry by morning. Late meals and slow digestion were taking their toll and the muted bangs of shutters and doors being pulled tight dulled but did not silence the commands issued between the Browns in their bedroom.

The next day Sarah's class finished early for a school trip Mrs B didn't wish her child to attend (something involving too much sun for Sarah's delicate complexion), and so she accompanied Kath to the café where she spent her afternoons while they waited for Rachel to finish. Sarah was thrilled to sit quietly at the table, observing and vibrating with excitement when Kath asked for *vino tinto* because it was what she'd heard someone else say and couldn't bear another moment not knowing what those ruby orbs felt like in the hand and in the mouth. Kath thought curiosity was always more dangerous than knowledge.

"They sent me a brochure through the post," Maria explained.
"Mmm-hmm."
Maria knew that Alex was often doing two or three other things when they spoke on the phone, but she retained enough information that it never felt like a waste of time phoning her. Mostly she did this to confirm a decision she'd already made but not said out loud.
"But the classes are all on weekday evenings."

"So get a sitter."

"I suppose I could."

"Well okay then." Alex was ready to move on, change topic.

"Did you say Aunt Kath used to be a nanny?"

"Um... yes I think, back in the day."

"I think she's in her sixties. Maybe seventy? I wonder if she'd like to meet the girls?"

"When? Why?"

"I *told* you about the letter, Alex. She's involved. I'll have to see her probably; I don't know, I'm just thinking out loud." But Alex was off, tripping down her own thought process.

"Christ she must have had a life. Her face is like a rock pool. Too much sun and too many fags. She definitely travelled. I bet she did, like, the Banana Pancake Trail before it was even a trail. I bet she backpacked. Did all that stuff. Can you even imagine what Thailand was like before *The Beach*? There must be places in the world that haven't been ruined by Americans yet."

Maria had learnt to let these moments of clarity from Alex run themselves out rather than trying to steer the conversation back to where it ought to be. She'd get bored eventually and start a new task like looking on Amazon Marketplace for second-hand mosquito nets and other things that definitely should only ever be bought new.

It was three days to go, and after the Browns had spoken of possibly extending her contract, when the regular waiter brought over her drink and began a stream of what Kath realised only halfway through was meant to be English. She leaned away as if from a loud noise, and gripped her bag close as she nodded weakly and waited for him to stop talking. When he finally did, Kath threw down more crumpled notes than necessary and bustled away. It was only that evening, after another bedroom argument, when Mrs B came into the sitting room and sighed, that Kath thought something might be going wrong.

"Well, darling," Mrs Brown said, a word Kath had never heard her use up until that point, "we didn't think you were this kind of girl, but Mr Brown has made up his mind." Her contract was terminated. Drinking alcohol, not to mention with Sarah in her charge, was inexcusable, "and would be, darling, if you were my own daughter." After a few more sighs, she patted Kath's icy hand, and then leaned over to whisper, "you'll sort yourself out, I'm sure." She handed her a final pay packet and left the room. In her room that night Kath sat at the open window and counted out the extra bills Mrs Brown had guiltily slipped in. If they could afford this, she thought, she should have been more ambitious from the start.

She stayed for only a week in Madrid, went back to the café with the intention of luring and then rejecting the waiter who had stood too close to her and said unintelligible things in broken English, but slept with him instead and woke up in his flat alone. She burnt coffee in his stove-top maker on purpose just to annoy him but then washed it clean when she worried he would just think her ignorant. In bed he'd been very energetic but everything he did was accompanied by a stream of foreign talk that made her feel like a set piece; she could take it or leave it, she thought.

At home she told no one she'd been sacked. She arrived with such confidence, as if she'd seen the world and understood it, that no one questioned her. The Browns never came back to town; they relocated somewhere further south and sent people and trucks to move their things rather than doing it themselves, which made Kath certain she should have taken them for all they were worth, and made her wonder if the *vino tinto* had just been a handy excuse to snip her out of the picture. She quickly realised there was a whole niche she'd been unaware of: people who had more money than they could ever spend and who'd had children in an offhand way, confident that wealth and leisure would take care of everything, especially infants. But her heart wasn't in it. One afternoon a man at the grocer's brushed an imaginary streak of flour off the back of her dress, and instead of pressing her lips together she told him the Spanish word for rear, one of the three words she'd picked up on that night with the waiter. Something had happened, come undone inside her, and she suddenly couldn't bear the dampness of the encroaching autumn and the blowsy wildflowers in gardens, the linen flapping in the wind on the day everyone did laundry because good weather probably wouldn't stick around. She wanted more cold drink, more wet heat in the eventual darkness of a summer night, more cool tiles underfoot and more accented shouts she couldn't understand in marketplaces and hot stone squares.

Alex made herself a drink and sat down to think. The letter from the lawyer had been followed up by another one, and this time Maria had taken two weeks to call. There were seven of them in total, great-nieces and great-nephews, or whatever you called the people who had a great-aunt. It wasn't that Alex didn't want five thousand pounds, or couldn't think of what to do with it. It was more that she couldn't imagine how their wizened old great-aunt had seven times that. Well, that needed no imagining; Maria had read that part of the letter a few times over the phone. Five thousand: it seemed slightly pathetic and glorious at once. Who would say no to it, but at the same time she could just... earn it at her job. It was a message more than a sum, a sign more than a winning. She could say no, add it to the pot for the rest of them. Maria, without being asked, had assured her it'd go straight into the girls' education fund because tuition was going sky-high and at this rate who would be left who could attend. "That's the point," Alex murmured, but otherwise didn't fill the silence when she left it hanging. Instead she thought of her own skin going powdery one day, her own closet filled with polyester and loud floral prints and shoes with fat black plastic soles, and how she wouldn't leave anyone a damn thing. *Drink till it's dry and then move on*, she thought, another one of her mottos that she flicked through like beads on a string when she needed to know what to do next. It worked this time like it always did. She drained her drink and started packing.

Kath had gone to Barcelona first and spent seven mornings in a café drinking cortados and feeling smug until she discovered she was incredibly bored. She met an Englishman with whom she travelled for a while, until he decided they should get married. He became furious when she balked, shouted at her that she should have "bloody well realised what was going on" and stormed out of the guesthouse they'd been staying in since arriving in Lisbon. He left behind his cigarettes, which she smoked one by one, propping her feet on the windowsill and feeling the breeze on her toes, exhaling towards the Atlantic. The next day she looked up nurseries and got a job teaching children to sing English songs three mornings a week. Her new headmistress was impressed by the names and locations she mentioned casually, and Kath wondered why everyone didn't live like this.

"Family responsibility, that's what brings us back," Aunt Kath said, sitting in a high-backed armchair and drinking a glass of ice water. It had been brought to her by a robust young man with a shiny name badge that declared he was "Douglas". She took it without acknowledging him and he retreated without turning his back, as if leaving a church. The cubes made a jocular, dainty sound as she drank a great hefty mouthful, crunching one cube forcefully with her back teeth. "My sister and I used to be close, you know. Oh, very close."

"I see. And she was ill so long." Maria had anticipated how awkward a face-to-face meeting would be, had gritted her teeth as she clasped her necklace and brushed the girls' hair before nagging them into the car. Trust Alex to vanish before everything was sorted. She'd known Aunt Kath knew about the will, about the little packets of money, which now seemed small enough that their only purpose was a roll call of sorts, a way to force everyone out of hiding, but didn't realise the extent of her involvement, the way she'd made herself something of a condition, a bridge to cross. The solicitor had informed her that Kath had actually been made the executor, which was both excessively cruel and completely arbitrary when she'd received nothing in the will herself. *Textbooks*, Maria had reminded herself as she backed the car down the drive. *Blazers. History trips to Belgium.* There was no graceful way for Maria to look her in the eye and collect her inheritance.

"I'd been away having adventures but I knew if she needed me I ought to come back. So I did," Kath said, her face hardening to a mask. At the front desk Maria had been told that occasionally she had episodes of anger, and Maria should simply come and find someone if it happened. She shouldn't take it personally; it was simply Kath's condition.

"Well, it's an important bond, isn't it. Nobody understands you like a sister," Maria purred, and nodded towards the girls playing in the hallway in a way that was meant to be knowing. She wondered if Alex would do the same for her. If anyone would. She couldn't imagine issuing a summons like that, or even living in a world where someone's misfortune turned into someone else's problem, but maybe that was her answer right there.

"I suppose it was my role to return, to care. For her, I mean." The mask was complete, fixed, and Kath rattled the glass like she was mad at it for being empty.

"Girls, girls come and say hi to Aunt Kath."

Maria's children shuffled their way over to the sofa, bickering over an old-fashioned wooden walking stick they'd found resting against a door. But Kath showed no interest in either of them.

"Keep yourselves busy for a moment while your mother and I talk." Kath gestured vaguely, away from her armchair.

"What are you talking about? If it's about us we really ought to listen. Plus it's rude to talk about someone whilst they're in the room. My teacher Mrs Simpson said so."

Kath held the girl's gaze. An ice cube, melting, shifted and clinked inside the glass.

Maria cleared her throat. "My eldest, so precocious," she said.

"Mmm," Kath agreed, looking at her. "Precocious. I know exactly what you mean."

Maria's youngest whispered something into her older sister's ear, behind the curtain of her blonde bob. Maria felt the tingle, familiar and unmistakable, all the way down her neck as if it was her own sister whispering in her ear. She watched her eldest stand there, defiant, while the other girl ran off to play in the garden.

Credits

An earlier version of "Blind Spots" originally appeared in the collection *Tip Tap Flat: A View of Glasgow* (2012); "The Reach of a Root" originally appeared at *Kenyon Review Online* (2013); "A Change Is as Good as a Rest" originally appeared in Issue 12 of *Gutter: The Magazine of New Scottish Writing* (2015); and "Woods for the Trees" originally appeared in *Short Fiction in Theory and Practice*, Volume 8 (2018).

Acknowledgements

Acknowledgements are due to the editors of the following publications in which some of these stories first appeared: *Gutter Magazine, Kenyon Review, Short Fiction in Theory and Practice*, and *Tip Tap Flat: A View of Glasgow*. We'd like to thank our friends, families and colleagues for their patience, support and advice. We would also like to thank Dana Keller for her keen editorial eye and Naghmeh Sharifi for her beautiful artwork.